What World is Left

MONIQUE POLAK

ORCA BOOK PUBLISHERS

Library and Archives Canada Cataloguing in Publication

Polak, Monique
What world is left / written by Monique Polak.

ISBN 978-1-55143-847-4

1. Theresienstadt (Concentration camp)--Juvenile fiction.
2. World War, 1939-1945--Children--Netherlands--Juvenile fiction.
I. Title.

PS8631.O43W43 2008   jC813'.6   C2008-902648-9

First published in the United States, 2008
Library of Congress Control Number: 2008927295

Summary: Anneke, a Dutch Jewish teenager, is sent with her family to Theresienstadt, a "model"
concentration camp, where she confronts great evil and learns to do what it takes to survive.

Orca Book Publishers gratefully acknowledges the support for its publishing programs provided
by the following agencies: the Government of Canada through the Book Publishing Industry
Development Program and the Canada Council for the Arts, and the Province of British
Columbia through the BC Arts Council and the Book Publishing Tax Credit.

Conseil des arts
et des lettres
Québec

Design by Teresa Bubela
Cover image used with the permission of the United States Holocaust
Memorial Museum, courtesy of Ivan Vojtech Fric
Additional photographs by Monique Dykstra
Author photograph by Elena Clamen

The views or opinions expressed in this book, and the context in which the
images are used, do not necessarily reflect the views or policy of,
nor imply approval or endorsement by, the USHMM.

ORCA BOOK PUBLISHERS   ORCA BOOK PUBLISHERS
PO Box 5626, STN. B   PO Box 468
VICTORIA, BC CANADA   CUSTER, WA USA
V8R 6S4   98240-0468

www.orcabook.com
Printed and bound in Canada.
Printed on 100% PCW recycled paper.
11 10 09 • 4 3 2

For Ma, with love

Acknowledgments

What World is Left could never have been written without the support and love of many people. I owe a huge debt to them all. Filmmaker Malcolm Clarke, director of the documentary *Prisoner of Paradise*, encouraged me to do the research for this book. When he learned that my mother had been a prisoner in Theresienstadt, he advised, "Make her tell you. Tell her she has to do it." Malcolm also put me in contact with Czech writer Eva Papouskova and filmmaker Martin Smok, who were of great assistance, both personally and professionally, when I traveled to the Czech Republic in the summer of 2007. Eva accompanied me on my visit to Theresienstadt, along with my friend Viva Singer from Montreal.

The Conseil des Arts et des Lettres du Quebec believed in this project and funded my research trip to Holland and the Czech Republic. Writer friends Claire Rothman Holden, Elaine Kalman Naves and Joel Yanofsky provided encouragement at various stages along the way. My neighbors Liz Klerks, Joanne Morgan and Don Kelly read the first draft of this book. The team at Orca Book Publishers—Bob Tyrrell, Andrew Wooldridge and Dayle Sutherland—brought the book to life. My editor at Orca, Sarah Harvey, was the midwife who helped me deliver it. Sarah, I can't thank you enough for your wisdom and sensitivity and for taking me where I had to go.

My daughter, Alicia Melamed, has always been my anchor and my sunshine both. My father, Maximilien Polak, helped in ways too numerous to mention, but his sense of humor is at the top of the list. My grandparents, Jo and Tineke Spier, remain with me in spirit every day and hovered close when I was working on this book. My husband, Michael Shenker, was with me every step of this difficult, exhilarating journey. But I owe the greatest debt to my mother, Celien Polak, who agreed to share her story after some sixty years of silence. Though my book's protagonist was inspired by my mother, Anneke's thoughts and feelings are entirely the product of my imagination. Sharing her story and allowing me the freedom to turn it into a work of fiction are my mother's greatest gifts to me and ones for which I will always be grateful.

One

My bed is warm and cozy. I think I'll sleep a little longer. I let my head sink into my feather pillow. The duvet feels so soft against my skin. I sniff the air. Yesterday was Thursday—laundry day. Sara, our new housemaid, hung out the sheets and pillowcases, and now they smell as sweet as the clover that grows by the canal behind our house.

I pull the sheets up so high they cover my face. A real Dutch face, Father often remarks when he looks across the kitchen table at my blue, blue eyes, my blond ringlets and my turned-up nose.

Tomorrow I will wear my favorite brooch, the one Johan gave me when I turned eleven. It is shaped like a tiny golden mirror with a curly handle on its end. I'll pin it on my new blue sweater from Opa, my grandfather, and all the other girls at school will admire my brooch and my new sweater.

I yawn; yesterday was such a busy day. What fun it was to go fishing behind the house with Father and Theo. I caught a striped perch, reeling him in all by myself, without Father's help. Theo, who is only ten, wanted a story, so I invented one about the perch. How his parents and his sister were caught by other fishermen and how he longed to join them on the land. "I'd rather be served for supper with a slice of lemon and a little mayonnaise," I said, pretending to be the perch in my story, "than have to swim here in the canal all by myself." Theo laughed at my imitation of the perch, and even Father seemed to enjoy the part about the lemon and the mayonnaise.

I yawn again and stretch my arms. But there's isn't room to stretch. In fact there's someone else—who can it be?—lying beside me. A girl I don't recognize.

At least not at first.

I want to push the girl away, but there isn't room. There's someone else next to her too. Oh, this is awful to be crammed so close.

And then I feel something bite the inside of my ankle. I reach down and swat at whatever it is.

That's when I realize where I am. Not in my warm cozy bed in Broek, the feather pillows fluffed, the sheets smelling like clover. I am in Theresienstadt.

I slap at my shoulder. Don't bedbugs ever sleep?

I shift my body and turn to face the other direction. At least Mother is next to me. Not all of the other girls are so lucky.

Because the lights—three incandescent bulbs hanging loosely from the ceiling beams—are always on in our barracks, I can see Mother's face. Even asleep, she looks tired. How long ago was it that she stood at the potbelly stove in our kitchen, wearing her apron with the tulips on it and frying up that perch I'd caught? "Butter," she'd said, adding another spoonful to the fry pan, "makes everything taste better."

I scratch the skin around my shoulder. I know I mustn't, but I can't help it. I am itchy everywhere. I fight the urge to jump out of the bunk. Besides, there is no place to go. We are prisoners here.

If only *this* was the dream, and I could wake up and return to my old life.

If I jump out of the bunk, I risk waking Mother, and then the other women will squawk. They are always squawking about something. "Don't make such a racket!" "Why does a girl your age have to use the bathroom so often?" "That's my peg you've hung your jacket on!"

I have to be careful not to bump my head. There are only a few centimeters of space above me. I hear rustling and the soft sound of someone else groaning in her sleep.

⁘☞

"Don't leave any spots. None at all."

"Yes, Frau Davidels," I call from inside my metal cauldron. The cauldron is so huge I had to climb on a chair and crawl into it. I've been scrubbing with a long wire brush for nearly half an hour, and the muscles on my arm are already sore. My whole body is damp with sweat. I hate cleaning.

But I know I mustn't complain. I was lucky to get this job in the diet kitchen in one of the camp's small infirmaries.

Cleaning toilets would be worse. My stomach turns at the thought of the long row of wooden latrines where I did my business this morning. To think that at home in Broek I minded having to share a bathroom with Theo. Now I have to squat next to at least a dozen other girls and women and wipe my bottom with scraps of torn-up glossy magazines.

"That's a good girl," Frau Davidels says, her voice fading as she walks down the corridor, supervising the others who work in the diet kitchen. Frau Davidels only pays compliments when there are no Nazis about. If there are Nazis in the diet kitchen, Frau Davidels' lips get small, and her voice turns sharp. "Scrub harder!" she tells us. "Can't you see that spot you've missed in the corner?"

Frau Davidels wears a white bonnet and apron. But because I've seen her when she isn't working, I know that underneath the bonnet, she has sleek dark hair that falls to her shoulders. Mother told me Frau Davidels is the widow of a Jewish Czech banker. I imagine the two of them, walking arm in arm down the cobblestone streets in Prague. It's a sunny day, and Frau Davidels is carrying a parasol.

Frau Davidels was sent to Theresienstadt with her only child, a son. But he was sent away on a transport. "The poor woman!" Mother said. "I don't know how she finds the strength to carry on. First the husband, then the boy. It's too much for one soul to bear." And so, when Frau Davidels uses her sharp voice, I try to remember how she must suffer. Doing that makes her sharp voice less hard to bear.

Transport. Just thinking the word makes me shiver and scrub harder. I didn't have to be in Theresienstadt long to understand that what everyone here fears most—more even than death itself—is finding a thin strip of paper with your name and number, and the word *Included!* on it—the sign that you are being sent on a transport. All I know for certain about the transports is that they are headed east. "To other ghettos like this one. Only better," the Czech gendarmes assure us. But something about the way the gendarmes refuse to look us in the eye when they talk about transports makes me suspect they are lying, trying to keep the lambs quiet before we are sent to slaughter.

Besides, if Frau Davidels' son was still alive, wouldn't he have written by now to tell her so?

The one goal—the only goal—at Theresienstadt is to keep your name, and the names of those you love, off the transport lists. But transports are as much a part of life here as bedbugs and latrines.

Father told Theo and me how Emperor Joseph II built Terezin in honor of his mother, the Empress Maria Theresa. How the old empress would turn in her grave if she knew what had become of her son's gift to her! It was the Nazis who renamed this place Theresienstadt.

Now it stinks of sweat and human waste. It is so crowded with prisoners there is no room to move about freely. And because trainloads of Jews keep arriving, others have to be shipped out.

I scrub at the crusty patch of black until it comes loose from the side of the cauldron and falls to the bottom. Considering the watery broth we get for lunch and dinner, it is a wonder the cauldrons get dirty at all. I look down at the little pile near my feet. Nothing but burnt crusts. I tried eating some on my first day in the diet kitchen, but the crusts tasted bitter, and they didn't make the hollowness in my belly go away.

"We're the lucky ones," Father told Theo and me when they pushed us out of the train at Buhosovice near Theresienstadt. "We're going to the model city."

Some model city! I shake out my arm to make the cramping go away. It is Father and Mother's fault we ended up here! How could they have been so foolish? Why hadn't we left Holland when it was still possible for Jews to leave the country? Parents were supposed to look after their children, but Father and Mother haven't done a very good job of it, have they?

Something inside my stomach does a flip. Only this time, it isn't hunger.

No, it's like the feeling I had at home when I went into Father's studio and opened one of his precious jars of paint. I dipped the tip of my finger into the thick red liquid and took a deep whiff of the paint. It smelled like chalk. Father seldom loses his temper, but he is very particular when it comes to his studio—and especially his precious art supplies.

"Who touched the magenta?" he called down in a booming voice. By then, Theo and I were at the kitchen table. Mother was at the stove, stirring a little sugar into the red cabbage and onions she was making for our lunch.

Theo shrugged. Mother pretended not to hear. At first I didn't say a word. But then I came up with an idea. The one person who wouldn't stand up for herself if I put the blame on her.

"It must have been Sara!" I called upstairs. At that point, Sara had been with us for about four months. She was Jewish and her parents had sent her from Germany when they felt the political situation there was becoming dangerous. They were sure she'd be safe in Holland. And Father and Mother had agreed to let her stay so long as she helped with the housework.

I knew it wasn't nice of me to blame Sara, but I did it anyhow.

"Sara!" Father's voice boomed even louder now. "I've told you before: never ever touch my paints!"

Sara must have been upstairs, changing the sheets on one of our beds. From downstairs, I couldn't make out her reply to Father. All I could hear was the sound of her voice as she apologized for something she hadn't done. At the time, I felt relieved. Better for Father to get upset with Sara than me. But now, scrubbing the cauldron, I wished I hadn't put the blame on Sara.

"Here's the scrubber, Hannelore. Make sure you get the cauldron perfectly clean. It's a matter of hygiene." Frau Davidels' voice takes me away from my memories of Sara: the way her fingers sometimes trembled when she dusted Father's books and how carefully she folded the laundry, rolling each pair of socks into a neat ball.

Who in the world is Hannelore? By now, I know everyone who works in the diet kitchen, but I've never met a Hannelore. I want to see her, to find out whether she is my age, but of course I can't see anything from inside my cauldron. And so my friendship with Hannelore begins before I even lay eyes on her.

"Hannelore," I whisper when I hear Frau Davidels' steps disappear down the tiled corridor.

At first, Hannelore does not answer. So I try again, only a little louder. "Hannelore, how old are you?" I ask.

When Hannelore finally speaks, she has a tiny voice that makes me think of a mouse. I wonder whether Hannelore has small dark eyes and a pointy chin. I hope she doesn't have a tail! And if she has one, I wonder how she manages to hide it under her clothes or what she does with it when goes to sleep.

"I'm fourteen," Hannelore answers from inside her cauldron.

"Me too!" I tell her, unable to hide my excitement. What were the chances we would be the very same age? It has been so long since I've had a friend to open my heart to. And if Hannelore is my age and works in the diet kitchen, we will certainly become friends. Best friends even. I imagine us lining up for soup together, huddling to keep warm. The guards will never let us link arms, but we can stand close to each other and exchange stories about the boys we like. I can tell her all about Franticek Halop. How handsome he is and how sometimes, when I pass him in the street, he smiles at me.

"My arm is tired," Hannelore says. Then she makes a sniffling sound.

"We're lucky to be here." My voice is sharper than I intend, but what surprises me most is how much I sound like Father. It could be him speaking from inside my cauldron. It's odd, because I hate Father's habit of turning everything into a lesson, and now I'm doing it myself. "They could have made us clean latrines," I tell Hannelore. "Scrubbing cauldrons is a pleasure compared to that."

Hannelore sniffles again. I'm not sure I can be friends with such a crybaby.

For a little while, all I do is scrub. I can feel my lips turning to a pout. This Hannelore has already disappointed me. She is the one to pick up our conversation. "Where do you come from?" she wants to know.

"Broek," I tell her, but then I realize she might not know where that is. I can tell from her accent that Hannelore is German. Perhaps she's never visited Holland. "Broek is in Holland," I tell her. "Not far from Amsterdam."

"I'm from Hamburg." Hannelore's voice sounds less tiny. "How did you end up in this place?"

"Girls!" Frau Davidels is back. I can hear someone else's footsteps too. It must be a Nazi supervisor. "No chatting!" Frau Davidels says. "Concentrate on your cleaning! Or else!"

I hear Hannelore sniffle. I imagine she isn't used to adults being stern with her. She must be a pampered girl. Maybe she is an only child, the long-awaited offspring of older parents. I can see them in my head. The mother is mousy. The father listens to Bach and smokes a pipe. They never raise their voices when they speak to her. No, Hannelore is their princess.

The way my mind works almost makes me laugh. "That Anneke is always inventing stories in her head," Opa, who is my father's father, used to say about me when he knew I was listening. He was teasing, but I know that in some way, he had paid me a compliment. I cannot paint like Father, but I can invent stories. And certainly that is something.

Two

 *H*annelore's question gets me thinking: How
did we end up in this place?

I reach up with the brush and scrub at a troublesome
bit of crust. We've been in Theresienstadt for only a
month, and already it is getting harder to remember
our old life. What brought us here, to this so-called
model city?

Of course they sent us here because we are Jews.
In my case, though, that seems particularly unfair.
Judaism means nothing to me. It's true I'm a Jew, but
I'm a Dutch girl, a Hollander first. I've never stepped
foot inside a synagogue, unless you count one visit to
the old, gray stone synagogue in Zutphen where my
opa lives. Theo and I only went there to see the stone
outside, the one that was laid by Isaac Van Raalte,
Opa's father, our great-grandfather. He was the last of
the religious Van Raaltes.

When Mother and I sometimes ran errands in
Waterlooplein, the part of Amsterdam where the
Orthodox Jews live, I felt as distant from them—with

their prayer shawls draped over their shoulders, the men with long side locks—as if they lived on Mars.

That is about all Judaism means to me. That and the dry crackers Mother sometimes offered us in springtime. "Matzoh," she called them. All I knew was that the crackers tasted awful until they were slathered with a thick layer of sweet butter and sprinkled with sugar.

Judaism is a subject I never thought much about before the war. I was too busy living my life, going to school, meeting up with friends and reading poetry. As for God—what need had I for Him?

Now that I'm in Theresienstadt, I've decided it's a good thing I was never a believer. Otherwise I'd have lost my faith in God. What kind of God would make the skin on an ordinary girl's fingers burn from scrubbing? What kind of God would invent latrines and guards with guns? No, I'm glad I have no faith to lose.

When we learned from Sara's family about the mistreatment of German Jews, we thought it was disgraceful, but we never worried for ourselves. Holland was far from Germany, and besides, wouldn't the many dikes on the coast of our little country keep us safe?

When we were younger, before Theo was old enough for school, the two of us would play in Father's studio while Mother prepared dinner. Father said he liked our company—as long as we didn't fight or meddle with his art supplies. Sometimes as a special treat, he let me change the water where he dipped his brushes. I'd walk down the hallway, carrying the little jar of water turned to blackish brown soup from the combination of all the colors Father had used. I remember feeling as important as if I were carrying the Holy Grail. What Jewish girl thinks such a thing? Not a religious one, that's for sure.

Sometimes, when Father's pen stopped making its scratching sounds and he laid his paint brushes aside, lining them up from shortest to tallest, Father would show us what he'd drawn that afternoon. Of course, it was really me he wanted to show his work to. Theo was too young to appreciate it.

The memory of one drawing comes to me now: a drawing that changed our lives. In it, a scowling man with a dark mustache climbs a stepladder. He is holding a paintbrush, and there is a can of paint by his feet. Underneath, in Father's tidy black script, are the words: *If only he'd stayed a housepainter.*

"The man's mustache is funny," Theo said when Father showed us the drawing.

"Who is he?" I asked Father. Father's drawings appeared from Monday through Friday on page three of the *Telegraaf*, the Amsterdam newspaper. His work was almost always funny, but this time, I didn't see the joke.

It was dusk, and a shadow crossed Father's face. "It's Adolf Hitler," Father explained.

"Hitler?"

"A madman who's come to power in Germany," was all Father said as he arranged his jars of paint in a neat row.

the end, our dikes did not keep us safe. In May of
1940, the Nazis, hungry to swallow up more of Europe,
invaded Holland. The *moffen*—that's what we called
the Germans because of the furry muffs they wore to
keep their hands warm in winter—came rolling in on
their big gray tanks like a herd of angry elephants. I was
almost too afraid to look. My knees shook when I heard
the rumble of the tanks. How could this be happening in
Holland? I'd studied wars in history class, but somehow,
I never dreamt I'd see one up close. Five days later,
Holland capitulated.

That was when Sara disappeared. Packed up her
little suitcase and left early one morning without even
bothering to say good-bye. She knew better than any
of us what the Nazis were capable of. Did she somehow
manage to escape from Holland? We never received
word from her, but I like to think she found a way out
of the country. I imagined her in London. I'd been to
Paris on holiday with my parents and Theo, but never to
London. Perhaps Sara had found work there as a housemaid, or fallen in love with a handsome widower who
spoke with a British accent. She loved his children as if
they were her own, and they called her Mama, nearly
forgetting their own mother who'd perished from some
terrible disease. Consumption, yes, it was consumption.
Such a tragedy.

There I went...inventing stories again.

Once the Nazis took power, life in Holland got worse and worse for us Jews. We were forbidden to enter public parks or visit Christian homes. I'll never forget the night we were turned away when we went for dinner to the Port van Cleef in Amsterdam.

"I'm so sorry, Meneer Van Raalte," Jan, the head waiter, told us, pointing to a sheet of paper tacked onto the restaurant's wooden door. A lump formed in my throat when I read the words on the sheet: *No Jews allowed.*

Jan refused to meet Father's eye. "Rules are rules," Jan said softly.

Mother turned her back and began marching down the street toward Central Station. "I'd prefer to eat beef steak at home anyhow," she called out.

"Yes!" I raised my voice so Jan would hear me. "And Mother's won't be dry like the ones you serve at the Port van Cleef."

Later, we would not be able to ride cars or trams, or even swim in the canal behind our house. Not being allowed to swim felt even more unfair than being turned away from the Port van Cleef. On hot summer afternoons, Theo and I listened from behind the curtains as the neighbor children splashed in the canal outside.

Then, of course, there was the yellow star with the word *Jood*—Dutch for Jew—inscribed on it in fierce black letters. Mother had to sew them on all our clothes, and we had to wear the star wherever we went. It had to be worn on the left side, where our hearts were.

I remember how hard my heart had beat the first time I wore one. Mother sewed it on my favorite blue sweater, the one from Opa's clothing shop in Zutphen. My eyes filled with tears. Not just because I had to walk around Broek with this humiliating mark, but because of how ugly it made my sweater look. The harsh yellow, a fiery angry shade, clashed with the beautiful blue.

None of us wanted to venture from the house wearing the star. Not even Father. It was Mother who was bravest. "I'm not going to stay cooped up inside all day," she announced, holding her head high. "I'm going for a walk."

We were waiting by the front door when she came back a half hour later. She gave us a bright smile. "That wasn't so bad," was all she said.

We got used to the yellow star. And though we were devastated at first, we also got used to it when the Nazis sent Father to a Dutch prison.

It turned out the Nazis didn't think much of the drawing Father had made of Hitler.

⁓⁓

Of course I missed Father. I was his favorite. And who would rub his forehead now when he got one of his migraines? Mother traveled once a week to the prison. When she got home, her face looked more tired than I'd ever seen it. "Father is fine," she assured us. "He'll be home soon." But it was almost a year before Father was released. In the meantime, I had to change schools. As a Jew, I was no longer allowed inside the Amsterdam Lyceum, the school I loved so much and where I did so well. Instead I was sent to the Joodse Lyceum—the Jewish High School—along with every other Jewish child my age who lived in the Amsterdam area.

The Joodse Lyceum was a plain, brown brick building in an inelegant part of town. How I longed for my old school!

I stopped trying to do my best. I left my homework undone in my satchel, and I whispered with the other students during class. "Anneke, if I have to tell you one more time to stop, I'll...," Meneer Cohen, who taught us Latin, warned.

I looked him in the eye. Everything about Meneer Cohen bothered me: the fact that he'd been a professor at the University of Amsterdam before the war, the gray stubble on his chin, his long tobacco-stained fingers, which shook when he got upset with us. Who was he to threaten me? He was as powerless as the rest of us.

"You'll...what will you do exactly, Meneer Cohen?" I said.

I'd never have dared to be so bold at the Amsterdam Lyceum, but what did I care now? Besides, what more did I have to lose? The other students giggled. But I took no pleasure in that. Most days, I hated Meneer Cohen. Sometimes, though, I pitied him, and that made me feel even angrier.

Johan was the only one I knew at the Joodse Lyceum. We'd been friends forever. My heart softened a little when I thought about the birthday party where he'd given me the golden brooch I loved so much. The day of the party seems so far away now, but what fun it had been. I could practically hear Mother's voice ringing from down the hall. "Johan's here!" she called. "The others are in the parlor," she told Johan.

I gave Wilma, Trude and Theo a stern look. If they laughed, they'd give our game away.

Johan was carrying a small parcel wrapped with a silver ribbon. "Happy birthday, Anneke," he said as he walked into the parlor. Mother was behind him, her eyes sparkling with mischief. She was the one who had taught us the game.

I had folded one of my legs beneath me, exactly the way Mother had shown me. My blue wool leotards felt scratchy. Before the party, Mother had cut the leg off another pair of my blue leotards and stuffed it full of rags, so that now, where my leg should have been, there was a stuffed leg in its place. Sitting like that was uncomfortable, but I tried not to squirm. The fun was worth a little discomfort. I tried not to laugh when I remembered how Trude shrieked when we played the trick on her.

"Johan! Johan! Pull on Anneke's legs!" Theo screamed with laughter. Though Theo was only eight at the time, he acted as if he was much younger. It comes from being the baby in the family.

"No, no," I said. "You have to pull on *all* our legs." I glared at Theo to remind him that if he weren't my brother, he'd never have been invited to this party.

Johan put his parcel down on the table. I wondered what it was. A bracelet or a brooch, perhaps? His mother has very good taste. Yes, I hoped it was a brooch. I would wear it on my new blue sweater.

Johan approached our little circle, kneeling so he could pull on each of our legs. Wilma giggled, which made Trude giggle. I held my breath so I wouldn't start giggling. Giggling can be contagious, especially at birthday parties where you play tricks on your guests.

"Oww, not so hard!" Theo said when Johan pulled on his leg.

Next he pulled on Trude's leg, then Wilma's. "It's a silly game," Johan said when he came to me.

I tried to look stern.

Johan pulled on my right leg first. I met Mother's eyes. She was standing by the door, smiling.

"Oh my God!" Johan screamed when he pulled on my left leg. The stuffed stocking came loose and fell to the floor. Johan covered his mouth with his hand. The rest of us doubled over in laughter.

❦

A little over a year later, I looked over at Johan, who was doing his math sums. So much had changed by then, but there was a little comfort in knowing that Johan was still Johan.

Not all of the four hundred or so students at the Joodse Lyceum were Dutch. About half were *moffen*, German Jews who'd fled to Holland as Sara had done.

One of the *moffen* girls caught my attention. Or rather her clothes caught my attention. She was far better dressed than the rest of us, and by then, with Father in jail, we had no money for luxury items like new clothes.

The girl's name, I learned, was Eva. We were the same age, but she was in another classroom. Eva's older sister, Ilse, had the same dark hair and eyes.

"I like your jacket," I told Eva one fall morning when I happened to be walking up the school steps next to her. The jacket had a gray fur collar. I think it was made of rabbit. I'd never seen anything so chic in all my life.

"Why, thank you," she replied, and I felt her eyes on my own outfit, sizing it up and finding it wanting. Mother had washed the blue sweater so many times it had started to pill. Little bits of blue wool dotted the elbows. Eva didn't return my compliment, but she slowed her pace so we could take the steps together.

"How do you find Meneer Cohen as a teacher? They say he can be very strict," she said.

"Strict?" I said, shrugging my shoulders. "He tries to be strict," I lowered my voice, and added, "but I think he's afraid of us."

Eva's dark eyes shone. "Afraid of you—of all of you?" she asked.

I nodded. "Especially of me. He's terrified of me!" I opened my mouth wide and made a roaring sound. Like a lion.

Eva giggled.

After that first conversation, we always waved when we saw each other from across the hall. And whenever we took the stairs together, I made my roaring sound and Eva would laugh appreciatively.

I tried to keep count of how many different outfits she had. A blue-and-black plaid skirt. A green sweater with buttons shaped like daisies. Blouses in every color. I decided that either her family was very rich, or Eva was very spoiled. Or maybe both. And though I was a little envious of her fancy clothes, I liked her because of her mischievous eyes and the way she laughed at my lion imitation.

Then one morning in June of 1942 Eva didn't come to school. I wondered if perhaps she'd come down with a cold or the flu. But Ilse was absent too. I swallowed hard.

Students often disappeared without a word from the Joodse Lyceum. Sometimes, we learned they were rounded up by the Nazis in one of their *razzias*—raids that were becoming more and more frequent—then sent away by train to be resettled in the east. Sometimes—and this was only the stuff of rumors—we heard that some of the disappeared students had gone into hiding. Usually, for safety, they would have to be separated from their families.

Poor Eva, I thought, knowing how attached she was to her sister. But then again, if her family was as rich as I imagined, they might have been able to stay together. I hoped that was the case, and for a moment, I wondered whether I could manage without Father, Mother and even Theo.

It's true that Theo could be a nuisance, and I sometimes wished he'd never been born, especially when he called me fat and said no boy would ever want to marry me. "You'll never find a volunteer!" he used to shout, laughing out loud and dancing around me in a circle. That made me so angry the vein in my forehead swelled up and made my head ache.

But no matter how annoying Theo was, I couldn't imagine waking up or going to sleep without him. Just thinking about it made my whole body go cold.

I so hoped Eva and Ilse and their parents were all together. And I couldn't help thinking: what good would Eva's fancy outfits do her now?

⚬

The notice that we were going to be deported from Amsterdam came in April, 1943. By then, Father was back home. Mother had petitioned for his release, and in the end, the Nazis decided their case against Father wasn't strong enough to keep him in prison any longer. It was a good thing the *Telegraaf* had continued paying Father's salary when he was in prison; otherwise, we wouldn't have had the money to pay our bills or to buy food.

When the news of deportation came, I felt at first like I was having a bad dream. Then I looked around our house and thought of all the things I'd miss: the stained glass window over our front door, the potbelly stove, the fireplace in the parlor and my lovely room. "How will I live without all the things I'm used to?" I sobbed.

"You'll manage," Mother said, running her hand across my forehead. "We'll all manage."

"At least," Father added, "the four of us will be together." That reminded me of the time he'd spent in prison away from us, and I was sorry then for having caused a fuss.

So I did my best under the circumstances. But you could tell things were tense at our house because Theo and I had stopped fighting.

We were each allowed to bring along one suitcase and a rucksack. Mother put a woolen blanket into each of our suitcases. She kept a close eye on whatever else we packed, shaking her head when she saw me tuck my volume of Heinrich Heine's poems into my bag.

"Don't you know those poems by heart, Anneke?" she asked. And because I did, I left the book on my desk. I packed two skirts, two blouses, two sweaters (including the blue one), and several pairs of socks and underwear. Only at the very last moment, when Mother was busy overseeing what Theo had packed and admonishing him for trying to bring along his model train, did I manage to pack two things Mother would no doubt have disapproved of: the mirror brooch Johan had given me, and my cream-colored silk dress with the smocking on it. Not that the dress fit me. In fact, I hadn't worn it since I was five. But it had always been my favorite. It had been custom-made by a dressmaker in Amsterdam and though I'd outgrown it nearly a decade before, I kept it at the back of my closet, refusing to pass it on to my cousin, Izabel. The dress was a memory of happier, carefree days.

I'd worn it the day I'd met Queen Wilhelmina. Well, all right, I didn't exactly meet her. But she'd seen me. Noticed me. There'd been a parade in Amsterdam on April 30 to mark her birthday. The streets were lined with Dutchmen, hoping to get a glimpse of her, perhaps to shake her hand. Even the red and yellow tulips blooming on the side of the road seemed to be reaching out to meet her.

I was sitting on Father's shoulders when Queen Wilhelmina passed. Mother was cradling Theo, who was only a baby, in her arms. The Queen's carriage slowed down when she passed us. First she nodded at Father and smiled. She must have known he was Joseph Van Raalte, the artist for the *Telegraaf*. Then she lifted her gaze in my direction. And I've never forgotten what she said then. "What a darling girl. And what a darling dress!"

Even then, with my bag nearly packed for our trip to God knew where, the memory of that day made me smile. And so, I slipped the little dress into my suit-case. If Mother lost her temper when she discovered it, so be it.

We were told to report to the *Hollandsche Schouwburg*, the only Amsterdam theater where Jews were still allowed inside. The day before, we made our way from Broek to downtown Amsterdam. We spent the night with Oom Edouard, Tante Cooi and their children. Their names had not yet appeared on the dreaded list.

There was little conversation at supper. Father and Oom Edouard discussed business. With whom had Father left the second set of keys to the house in Broek? Which farmer had agreed to hide Father's car, his precious Delahaye, in his barn? What did his editors at the *Telegraaf* have to say, and would they continue to look after Father's bills during our absence?

After dinner we gathered in the parlor. Mother reached into her rucksack. I supposed she had some spices for Tante Cooi, or perhaps her apron with the tulips. Instead, Mother pulled out a flannel sheet. Something porcelain was wrapped inside. Mother's Delft teapot perhaps?

I nearly stopped breathing when I saw what it was. Not Mother's teapot or spices or an apron. No, it was my porcelain tea set. The one I'd served tea in to Wilma and Trude when we were little. Why had Mother brought it here?

Mother looked at me. "Anneke," she said, "I knew you'd want Izabel to have your tea set." She must have noticed my face turn red. I was so angry I thought I might explode. "Izabel will look after it while we're away. Won't you, Izabel?"

Izabel got up from the horsehair chair where she was sitting and stepped toward the tea set. My tea set.

But I got there first. I tore the tea set from Mother's hands. Once I had it, my hands shaking with fury and sorrow and the injustice of it all, I took the tea set and hurled it down the stairway that led up to the apartment. The teapot and the cups and saucers made a clinking crashing sound as they hit first the wall and then the floor.

Hot tears began to fall down my cheeks, but I didn't cry out. I had no words for how unhappy and afraid I felt. Everything was being taken away from me! Everything!

Mother raised her hand to her mouth. "Anneke, what have you done?" she asked.

Only Father seemed to understand. When I looked at him, I saw his eyes were filled with tears. He looked at my mother. "Let Anneke be," he said.

Three

We had to be at the *Hollandsche Schouwburg* at eight the next morning. It would take forty minutes to walk from Oom Edouard and Tante Cooi's apartment. We'd never manage it with our suitcases and rucksacks. And by then, Jews were no longer permitted to ride the trams.

So Father telephoned Muidermann. Muidermann used to come to our house in Broek to fetch Father's sketches and deliver them to the *Telegraaf* office in Amsterdam. Mother sometimes rewarded Muidermann with a syrup waffle or a piece of *gefulde koek*—cake filled with marzipan. But today there wouldn't be any sweets for Muidermann.

He arrived twenty minutes later with his horse and flatbed wagon. Muidermann kept his eyes on the cobblestone street as the four of us sat together on the flatbed, our suitcases piled high behind us. We drove in silence to the *Hollandsche Schouwburg*. The streets were empty, and Muidermann's horse whinnied when a crow flew by. Mother and Father held hands.

I only turned around once to take a last look at the streets of Amsterdam. Even in the half-light, it was a beautiful city. I'd come here to go to school and to run errands with Mother. But I never dreamed that I would have to leave like this. My heart felt heavy in my chest. In the distance, I saw the Amstel River. Somewhere beyond that was our home in Broek.

I wanted to cry, but I knew it would only make things worse for Mother and Father and Theo. So I bit down so hard on my lip I tasted blood. Would I ever see my little room under the rafters again?

⁓⁓⁓

I never heard such wailing or saw such confusion as when we pushed open the heavy wood door to the *Hollandsche Schouwburg*. A white-haired boy cried for his mother. An old man with only one leg peered around the hall. "A German war veteran," Father whispered. All I could think of was the stuffed leg game we'd played so long ago at my birthday party.

"Keep moving!" an angry voice commanded us. When I turned to see who it was, I saw a Nazi soldier with a rifle tucked under his arm. For a moment, I froze. I'd never seen a gun up close before. If the soldier got any angrier, he might shoot at us! I could practically hear the sound of the bullet whizzing through the air. I drew closer to Mother and Father.

"Keep moving, Jews!" the soldier barked. And we did.

In all, there were over three hundred of us. There were other German war veterans who'd come to live in Holland. "Look!" Theo said excitedly, pointing to a tarnished medal hanging from an old man's jacket. "That one has an Iron Cross!"

Mother squeezed my hand. "It's a good sign we're with him," she said, lifting her eyes toward the man with the Iron Cross. "The Nazis would never harm one of their own war heroes. Not even if he was a Jew."

I hoped she was right.

In early afternoon, we were loaded onto the train. The seats had been removed so more of us could be crammed into each wagon. I sat on my suitcase, huddled between Theo and Mother. From outside, I heard a heavy thud as the doors slammed shut and then the snap of a padlock. There was no way out now. I looked at the anxious faces around me and my chest tightened. We were trapped.

The train jerked once, then twice, before it pulled out of the station.

I don't know exactly how long we traveled. At first I looked up at the windows. I had to crane my neck from my spot on the floor. Outside I saw green fields and blue sky with an occasional puff of cloud. How was it the countryside could stay the same when our lives were changing so irrevocably? Later, we passed golden fields. Their brightness hurt my eyes. "Coleseed," Father told me. "Beautiful, isn't it?" His voice seemed to be coming from far away.

But I knew what Father was thinking: that he'd like to draw the coleseed fields, capture them on paper. He often brought his sketchbook along when we went fishing in Broek. A few scratching sounds, then the sound of crumpled paper—Father was seldom happy with his first attempts—and then there was a sketch. A cow passing by a tulip field. A farmer wearing a straw hat, sitting atop his tractor.

Some people thought drawing came easily to Father. "Quite the job you have, Meneer Van Raalte," I'd heard one of our neighbors say to Father. "One small drawing and then your workday is done. A butcher like me has to slave behind the counter all day long." But I knew the truth: Every image Father produced required careful, painstaking work. I wondered when he would be able to draw again.

Soon we lost interest in what we could see from the train windows. All that mattered was emptying our bladders—and eventually, more than that. At first I tried to ignore the heaviness building below my navel. Don't think about it, I told myself. But every time the train bumped against a rail, I remembered what I was trying so hard to forget.

There was no bathroom. Only a rusty tin bucket, dented in the middle. The man with the Iron Cross had already used it. I averted my eyes when I heard him loosen his trousers. He wasn't the only one to use the bucket. Soon, the wagon reeked of urine—and worse. I tried not to gag.

On the train, the adults argued about where we were headed. "We're going to a model city," said a woman who wore her hair in a tight gray bun. Her husband walked with a limp: another German war veteran. The woman pulled a brown envelope from her purse. "See," she said, "we've bought ourselves land in the model city. They told us we'll have a beautiful view of the countryside."

A young man scowled. "You've wasted your money. They're sending us to the ovens," he said.

Mother put her hands over Theo's ears. "Don't listen," she told us.

"Aren't you Joseph Van Raalte?" a woman asked Father.

Father looked pleased. He loved it when people recognized him. "Yes, I am."

"I so admire your drawings."

"Thank you," Father said. He shrugged his shoulders as if he was shaking off the compliment.

The man with the scowl looked up. "That drawing you made of Hitler on the ladder landed you in some trouble, didn't it?" he asked.

When Father nodded, I sensed his mind was drifting far away, perhaps back to the Dutch prison where he was kept in solitary confinement. "In these times," he said a moment later, "drawing can be a dangerous business."

Eventually the combination of the conversation, the terrible odors and the way we were crammed into the wagon began to wear me down. "I can't bear it anymore!" I whimpered. "It stinks in here!" My whimper turned to a scream.

The woman who recognized Father turned away.

Theo started whimpering.

"Let me out of here!" I cried.

Father's shoulders tensed. I could tell he didn't know what to do.

Mother clamped her hand over my mouth. I tried to push her hand away, but she wouldn't let me. "Anneke," she said sternly, meeting my eye, "stop it. Stop it now. You're only making things worse. Think of Theo. Set an example for your little brother."

I swallowed my tears. Of course Mother was right. There was no use in making a fuss. I was only making things worse. I stared down at the floor. And I tried to ignore the foul odors of the wagon.

Hours passed and turned into days. The misery of the journey wore me out, and finally I managed to get some sleep. It was dark when the train finally sputtered to a halt. I didn't know how long I'd slept. My tongue felt furry, and I'd drooled on Mother's shoulder. There were dark rings of sweat under her armpits.

"*Raus! Raus!*" German voices called. "Get going! Get going!"

Dogs barked.

Father helped Theo and me to our feet. I held my nose

as I passed the stinky pail. Anything would be better than this crowded wagon.

Outside it was pitch dark, but the Nazi soldiers who were urging us to hurry up were carrying lanterns, which gave off an eerie light. I could just make out a road, lined with tall, spindly, poplar trees.

"Where are we going?" Theo asked.

"They're taking us into the forest. Like Hansel and Gretel," I told him.

"But we don't have pebbles to mark the way," Theo said in a sleepy voice. In the dark, I could see the dogs' fangs and the long shapes of rifles, hanging from the soldiers' sides. The soldiers pointed in the direction of a narrow road. "*Raus! Raus!*" Was that all they could say? And then, as if in answer to the question I'd just asked myself, one of the Nazis added, "*Juden schwein!*"

My back stiffened. How dare he call us that—Jew pigs! Father, who was walking on my left, must have noticed my reaction. "Stay calm," he whispered. "It's only words. Remember what's important—"

"That we stay together," I said, finishing Father's sentence.

"I'm getting blisters on my heels and on one sole," Theo whimpered after we'd been walking in the dark for a quarter of an hour.

Father sighed. He had a suitcase in either arm; he couldn't carry Theo too. "You'll just have to keep walking," Father told Theo.

"We're nearly there," Mother said. She had my suitcase and Theo's. Each of us was responsible for our own rucksack. Mine chafed again my back. I could feel the skin breaking underneath.

Someone behind me made a crying sound. "I can't go on. I'm too tired." It was the woman who wore her hair in a gray bun.

"You must go on," her husband told her. "Don't you want to see our new property?"

"Bah!" she said. "All lies. Nothing but lies."

I sucked in my breath. If this woman had given up hope, what did it mean for the rest of us?

The light from a lantern shone ahead, landing on a spot at the side of the road. When a Nazi soldier laughed, the sound was hard, almost metallic. There seemed to be a pile of abandoned rucksacks by the curb. But when we got closer, I saw two crumpled lifeless figures, huddled together.

I covered my mouth with one hand. These people were dead, their lives snuffed out like candles. They had been walking on the road like we were now, and then they'd died. Collapsed, perhaps, or shot by the Nazis. I shivered with terror. What would happen to us? Might we also end up dead by the side of the road?

"Keep moving!" the soldier shouted. He shone his lantern on the pair of corpses. "Unless you'd like to join their party." This time, when he laughed his metallic laugh, the other soldiers laughed too.

We finally stopped at a building called the *Schleuse*. It had long narrow windows that looked like gaping eyes. *Schleuse* was the German word for floodgate, but at that point, we didn't yet understand why this ugly building had been given that name. All we knew was that this was where the Nazis had directed us, prodding us with wooden sticks as if we were cattle. We were learning quickly that it was best to do whatever they wanted.

One woman I recognized from the *Hollandsche Schouwburg* had dared complain. "Don't push me!" she said in Dutch to one of the Nazis. Her reward for speaking up had been a sharp slap in the face. Hours later, her cheek still bore traces of the Nazi's handprint. When I thought about the rifle he was carrying, I bit my lip. No, it was best to follow orders.

There were fewer Nazis inside the *Schleuse*. Here, other prisoners—Jews like us—were in charge, though they in turn were supervised by Czech men in uniform. These were the gendarmes.

The four of us went to stand at the end of a long line. When Theo leaned against my leg and began to doze off, I didn't push him away. Up ahead, a tired-looking man with sunken cheeks sat at a desk, taking notes as he interviewed each new arrival. Once people finished with him, there was another line. Would we ever get to sleep?

"Spiegel," I heard the man in front of us say when he reached the desk. "Israel Spiegel and my wife Mathilde."

The man at the desk nodded as he recorded the information. "Dates of birth, place of residence and occupation," he said, without looking up.

"Van Raalte," Father said when it was finally our turn. "Joseph, Tineke, Anneke and Theodoor." His voice shook when he listed our birthdates and place of residence. "I'm an artist in Amsterdam. I work for the newspaper." Father's voice got a little stronger. Describing his work seemed to give him courage.

"It's full of artists here, and musicians and architects," the man behind the desk said.

"And men without legs," added Theo, who was awake again.

"Yes," the man said with a sigh, "and men without legs." Then he lowered his voice so the gendarme behind him wouldn't hear. "And men without hearts. Like Commandant Rahm."

Mother gasped. Father leaned in toward the man. "Tell me," he whispered, "is it possible to survive here?"

I edged in a little closer. I had to hear the man's answer.

He wrote something on his sheet, but I knew from the lines on his forehead that he was considering Father's question. "It's possible," he said at last, "but not likely."

I felt like I might topple over. Not likely? But I was too young to die! I hadn't yet begun to live. Would I never fall in love or have children of my own?

Mother squeezed my hand. Her palm felt damp.

The man behind the desk raised his eyes to Father's. "To survive," he said under his breath, "you'll need to be very smart."

And for the first time in many weeks, I felt a tiny ray of hope. After all, there was no one smarter than Father.

※

The real floodgate came once we joined the second line. Up ahead—it was too dark to see much—we heard the sounds of suitcases being unbuckled and of crying. "Those were my grandmother's Sabbath candlesticks," a woman whimpered.

"You won't be needing them here," a voice answered, and then there was a crashing sound as the woman's candlesticks were thrown to the floor. For a moment, I remembered the tea set I hurled down the stairs and the shards of porcelain Mother swept up afterward.

Mother didn't say a word when our turn came, and they took her gold wedding ring. They took Father's wedding band and his watch too. But he only went pale when they confiscated his sketchpad and three tiny jars of paint. One was red, one yellow and one blue. They were the primary colors and with them, Father could make any color.

Even before the gendarme opened my suitcase, I knew I'd lose my brooch. So I watched in silence as he tore it loose from my blue sweater and threw the tiny golden mirror into the pile. It landed without a sound. I turned away.

With rough hands, the gendarme fumbled through the rest of my belongings. I'd hidden my old silk dress inside a cotton coat so Mother wouldn't know I'd packed it. The fact that the gendarme didn't find the dress made up a little—but just a little—for my brooch.

Four

"You're not the least bit mousy," I blurt out when Hannelore climbs out of her cauldron.

Her face is shiny with sweat, and her hands are raw from scrubbing, but Hannelore is no mouse, despite the way she whimpered before. Hannelore grins. "You expected a mouse?" she asks.

Hannelore has long dark braids, the color of my favorite semi-sweet Droste chocolate, and though her eyes are dark, they aren't mousy. "I've discovered something new about myself today," she announces, dropping her scrub brush and putting her hands on her hips.

"What's that?"

"I've discovered I have a talent for scrubbing. Come have a look!"

I follow Hannelore up the narrow wooden ladder that leads up to her cauldron and peer down into it. She is right. She has done a fine job. Especially for her first day. I whistle. "You're quite the scrubber, you are," I tell her. "A gold medal scrubber. Too bad scrubbing isn't an Olympic sport!"

"Just don't tell my mother," Hannelore says, turning her head both ways to indicate that what she is about to say is top secret. "Or else she'll have me scrub at home too." Then Hannelore's dark eyes seem to turn a shade darker. "That is, if we ever go home."

"Of course we'll go home," I say, a little too quickly. Though I've only just met her, something about Hannelore makes me feel like I have to protect her. "Haven't you heard," I ask her, "that the war is almost over?"

"Says who?" When Hannelore shrugs, the gesture reminds me of an old woman.

"I heard some of the men say so."

"Prisoners?" Hannelore asks.

I nod.

Hannelore shrugs again. "That's what they need to tell themselves. But I don't believe it. Not for a second."

When Frau Davidels comes down the hallway, Hannelore makes that sniffling sound again. "We mustn't upset her," she whispers.

But there are no Nazis around, and Frau Davidels smiles when she sees Hannelore and me together. She draws us close to her. "It helps to have a friend," she says, "especially during hard times." Then without saying a word, she drops something into my apron pocket, and then something into Hannelore's.

The door swings open, and we hear the *click-click* of a Nazi officer's boots.

"Be off! And mind what I say!" Frau Davidels tells the two of us, her voice suddenly businesslike again.

We climb back into our cauldrons and do not say a word until the officer disappears down the hall.

"A potato!" Hannelore whispers breathlessly.

"It's one of the bonuses that comes from working in the diet kitchen," I tell her. "See, you were wrong about Frau Davidels. There's no need to be afraid of her. Maybe you're also wrong about the end of the war."

Hannelore is quiet. I imagine she is patting the potato in her pocket. "Wait until I show this to Mother!" she says.

Sometimes the potatoes Frau Davidels gives us are blackened or mushy, but that doesn't matter. They are still prizes. Boiled up in a little water, they make a chunky broth that is far more substantial than the watered-down lentil soup we get for lunch and dinner.

On our way back to the barracks—it turns out Hannelore and her mother are housed in the same barracks as Mother and me—we pass a group of old people waiting on the cobblestone street. Because it's June they have no need for warm clothes. Their arms are almost as thin as tree branches.

The old people pounce when a prisoner comes by dragging a wheelbarrow behind him.

"What are they after?" Hannelore asks as we watch the old people stuff their pockets.

"Potato peels," I say.

Hannelore makes a gulping sound. I know she is remembering the potato in her pocket. Again I get the feeling that Hannelore needs looking after. "Never mind," I tell her, tugging her wrist.

Though Hannelore and her mother sleep at the other end of the dark musty barracks, I feel better knowing Hannelore is there.

I can never decide what time of day is worse at Theresienstadt—bedtime or morning. At night, I huddle next to Mother, but then the bedbugs begin to gorge on us. They are, it seems, as hungry as we prisoners. I slap at the bugs, and the sound of my slapping joins together with all the other slapping in the women's barracks, making a kind of chorus. If it weren't so pitiful, it might be funny.

The bit of wall behind our bunks is smudged with brownish red from the bloody fingerprints of other women who've smacked at bedbugs and fleas. This is one war we'll never win.

If only bedbugs and fleas could write. Then we could make them sign a treaty and leave us alone. It's a silly thought, I know, but it helps me forget the bedbugs and fleas, for a few moments at least.

I miss Father most at night. At home in Broek, I used to wait for him to knock on my door and kiss me good night. Now he and Theo are in another barracks several streets away. We can only be together as a family for half an hour on Sunday afternoons. Though I'll never admit it to anyone, I even miss Theo.

Mornings bring their own misery. Waking up even hungrier than I was when I went to sleep is bad enough. But the worst is that very first moment when I wipe the sleep from the corners of my eyes, and I remember where I am. That is worse even than the hollowness in my belly.

One morning my throat is very sore. It hurts to swallow. The lines around Mother's eyes deepen when she feels my forehead. "You have a fever," she tells me. "You can't work in the diet kitchen today."

"I have to work." My voice sounds rough. When I crawl out of the bunk, all my joints ache. Even joints I never knew I had.

We both know that in Theresienstadt, not reporting to work can be dangerous. Mother, who has a job in the central kitchen distributing soup, has told me how the supervisors there keep detailed records about each worker: start time, end time, number of absences. "Too many absences," she explained, "could land a person on a transport." The memory of her words makes me jump down to the wooden floor. When my feet hit the ground, my throat throbs even more. But I have no choice: I have to go to work.

But then I feel my knees cave beneath me. Everything around me—the straw mattresses on the lowest bunks, the other women scrambling to get dressed—suddenly turns blurry.

Some other prisoners have to help Mother drag me back to my sleeping spot. Someone else gets my enamel cup and goes to fill it with a little water. Even taking small sips hurts. "You have to drink, Anneke," Mother says. "And no work today. I'll talk to Frau Davidels." Then she kisses my forehead and sighs.

I must have dozed off because when I awaken, the barracks is completely empty. All its occupants are at work, doing whatever they must to stay alive. Some are cleaning, some are cooking, some are sewing. All of them are supervised by Nazi officers who will not let them take a break or stretch their legs. It is dark when the women leave for work, and it will be dark when they return to the barracks at the end of the workday.

Little rays of sun peep through the narrow cracks in the walls. It must be mid-morning by now. I swat at a bedbug. If I had more strength, I'd get up and shake out my blanket. That is one way, at least, to get rid of some of the pesky creatures.

It is better to sleep than to battle the bedbugs. I kick the blanket off. It's rough and scratches my skin. Besides, I'm too hot for it anyhow.

The barracks have grown darker. "Anneke, have some more water." It is Mother. She holds a tin cup to my lips. "Hurry," she says. "I told them my period started, and that I needed to come back to the barracks for a cotton rag."

I prop myself up against the wall and take a few sips.

"I'm feeling better," I tell her. It isn't true, but the words make Mother smile. I'd nearly forgotten the way her face changes when she smiles, the way her blue eyes shine and her chin dimples.

When Mother leaves, I begin to wonder whether she was ever here, or if, in my fever, I dreamt she'd come to check on me. But my throat feels less parched, and I spot the tin cup near my knee. No, Mother has definitely been here, and she brought me water. She told me how she used her period for an excuse.

I've only had one period. It came shortly before we left Holland. I hadn't thought anything of it when I awoke one morning with an achy belly. But when I noticed the smear of blood in my underpants, I had quite a shock. How could I be bleeding from down there?

At first I was too ashamed to tell Mother. But when the bleeding got heavier, I knew I had no choice. We'd probably have to fetch the doctor.

"Mother," I called from the toilet. "I have a problem."

Theo must have been nearby. "Anneke has a problem! Anneke's in the toilet and she has a problem!" he jeered from the hallway.

"Go away, you idiot!" I told him, my temper suddenly flaring.

Father came down from his studio to see what the fuss was about. I heard him lead Theo up the stairs. When they were halfway up, Father stopped. I could hear the oak floorboards creak with his weight.

"Anneke," he said in a stern voice, "that was no way to speak to your brother."

Mother didn't think we needed the doctor. Instead, her face brightened and she laughed. "My goodness," she said, "my little girl is growing up. Becoming a woman." And then, as she reached into the bottom drawer for some strips of cotton, she explained about periods. How they were perfectly natural. How it meant that one day, I'd be able to have children of my own and make her a grandmother.

"Are you having cramps?" she asked gently.

When I nodded, she sent me back to my bed. Then she brought me a hot water bottle wrapped in a flannel sheet and laid it on my belly.

But I haven't had a period in the two months I've been at Theresienstadt. People say it is because we don't get enough to eat. I know I've lost weight because I can feel my hipbones jutting out below my waist. Sometimes, when I'm scrubbing a cauldron and there is time to think, I worry that maybe I won't ever be able to bear children. The thought makes me want to weep.

I haven't asked Mother if she still gets her period. Maybe it is different for grown women.

When I wake up again, the barracks is even darker, and Hannelore is perched on the edge of my bunk. "Frau Davidels warned me not to come too close," she says, running her hand along my arm. Her touch feels cool. "But she sent me to see whether you were feeling any better."

"I need to pee," I tell Hannelore. "But I don't think I can manage on my own."

"That's what friends are for," Hannelore says as she helps lift me from the bunk.

I lean on Hannelore as I stumble to the latrines. Not even the chlorine and lime that are sprinkled regularly into the pits help mask the stench.

"It's a shame I have a sore throat. A blocked nose would be handy just now," I tell Hannelore. Because it hurts to laugh, I only laugh a little when I say so.

"That's you, Anneke," she says. "Always making light of things. We couldn't be more different, could we?"

Hannelore kneels down and holds onto my arm while I squat over one of the holes. Afterward, she hands me a square of magazine so I can wipe myself. "Have you seen him lately?" she whispers as she walks me back to the barracks. We are approaching the central square in the middle of Theresienstadt. Out of habit, we press toward the narrow walkway on the side. Jews are not permitted to enter the square.

"No, not since last week," I tell her. Just as I imagined I would, I've told Hannelore all about Franticek Halop, and once I even pointed him out when we were standing in line for soup. Franticek is easy to spot because of his height and his shock of dark curly hair.

"Isn't he too old for you?" Hannelore asked. I could hear the disapproval in her voice. "He must be at least eighteen."

"Twenty. And not only that. He has a girlfriend!" I said, enjoying Hannelore's shocked expression—the way her dark eyebrows rose and then knitted themselves together.

"Anneke, how could you let yourself like a boy like that?"

"I can't help it," I said, trying to explain. "He's as handsome as a prince. I like everything about him—even the way he smiles."

Hannelore doesn't have eyes for any boy in the camp. She is still in love with Gunter, a Christian who lived on her street in Hamburg. "After *Kristallnacht*, the night the Nazis destroyed our synagogues," she told me, "most of our Christian neighbors wanted nothing more to do with us. Even those we'd known for years. But not Gunter and his parents. They brought us food and tried to warn us about Nazi raids. Gunter walked me to the train when we left for here. He said he'd wait for me." Hannelore's dark eyes grew misty.

"Did you kiss him?" I wanted to know.

Hannelore flushed.

"I suppose that means yes," I said, and we both laughed.

.·ö⁀

A group of Nazis is marching down the middle of the square, headed toward us. The buckles on their boots gleam in the afternoon sun. They march in perfect unison as if they are listening to the beat of some faraway drum.

"We'll say I helped you use the latrine. That you're ill, and I'm taking you back to the barracks before I return to the diet kitchen." Hannelore's voice is shaking.

"We haven't done anything wrong," I tell her.

Hannelore stops walking. For a moment, she looks me in the eye. "Who of us here has done anything wrong?"

But the Nazis pay no attention to us. They have other business to attend to. From the corner of the street where our barrack is, we watch as they continue their march.

"Please, please. No!" we hear a man wail.

And then the familiar "*Raus! Raus!*"

My stomach clenches.

Soon, there are more pleading voices and what sounds like a gunshot. My whole body stiffens with fear. So does Hannelore's. But still, we are curious. Holding onto each other tightly, Hannelore and I cross the street so we can get a better look. In the distance, we can see the Nazi soldiers we spotted earlier. Only now they've stopped marching. They have rounded up three men and are leading them down one of the side streets. Three Jews. One of them is bald. Like Father.

Things start to look blurry to me again, the way they did in the morning when I got down from my bunk. It's as if I can feel my heart beating in my throat.

"Are they taking them to the *Kleine Festung*?" I manage to ask Hannelore. The *Kleine Festung*, or Little Fortress, is located just outside of Theresienstadt. It is where prisoners are taken when they break the camp rules. But Father hasn't broken any rules. At least none that I know of.

"I don't think so," Hannelore says.

"What if that bald man is my father?" I whisper. My forehead feels even hotter than it did when I got up this morning.

Hannelore doesn't lift her eyes from the scene ahead of us. "Of course they don't have your father. Your father's a famous artist. He's on the list of prominent prisoners. They're protected—for now at least."

I feel the tension begin to drain out of me. Hannelore is right. The man with the bald head can't be my father.

"Look, look!" Hannelore says. I gasp as I watch and listen. There is shouting, muffled cries and then an eerie silence. Two of the Nazis hoist the three prisoners onto a plywood platform. I can hardly breathe.

"They're hanging them!" Hannelore is nearly shouting. Her dark eyes look like they're about to pop out of her head.

I turn my head away. I've seen the wooden gallows on one of the smaller squares near the main one. But I have never seen it in use, always believing it was just another way of frightening us prisoners, of making sure we followed orders.

I try to concentrate on the dust motes floating near my knees. I am afraid to look up. There are so many dust motes. I try counting them. Eighteen, nineteen... Where do dust motes come from? My head feels heavy from so much leaning down. Count the dust motes, I tell myself. Don't look up.

"One man's tongue is hanging out of his mouth. It's purple. Like a dog's," Hannelore says. Her voice is quieter now, but I can tell she's angry.

I still refuse to look up. "You can't possibly see that from here," I whisper.

It is not until nighttime that we learn why the three men were hanged. One did not tip his hat when a Nazi officer passed. One tried to smuggle a letter to his wife. And one stole a potato. I wonder whether he was the one with the bald head—and the purple tongue.

If only I could cry. I'd cry for those three dead men, and also for myself and for Hannelore who watched them die.

But my throat hurts too much. It's as if the tears I cannot cry have settled at the bottom of my throat and are making it throb.

Five

It is a sticky August afternoon. Even the flies are struggling in the heat, buzzing with less vigor than usual. By now, after four months in the camp, I've almost stopped thinking about our claw-foot bathtub in Broek. The closest I've come to a bath is the occasional pail of gray water and a waxy piece of soap that doesn't lather when I use it. The smell of sweat—mine and everyone else's—permeates the air. And like all the other indignities, after a while, I hardly notice it anymore.

Mother and I are packing our satchels. I haven't told Hannelore about our new living arrangements. I feel too guilty about leaving her behind in the barracks. After all my good fortune, for that's what it feels like, all has to do with my father. Hannelore's father died before the war. "It's just as well he didn't live to see what happened to his beloved Germany," Hannelore told me when she spoke about him. Now it is just her and her mother and a frail uncle, who is housed in one of the men's barracks.

We are moving to our own quarters on Jagergasse, a narrow alley three blocks behind the main square. Best of all, Father and Theo are coming too.

When we meet them at the front door of our new home on Jagergasse, I feel as if I might fall over from happiness. Father's face is thin and Theo's skin is sallow, but we are together again.

For a moment, I think of Hannelore and the spot in the barracks where she sleeps. Tonight, some other girl will lie in my old spot. The women's tongues will wag when they realize Mother and I are gone. When they learn we have moved to Jagergasse and are together with Father and Theo, the women will wonder how we managed to secure such an arrangement.

No doubt some of them will say we should have stayed in the barracks with them to show our solidarity. Part of me wonders how things would be different had Father refused the Council of Elders' offer of the quarters on Jagergasse.

The Council of Elders is the group of prisoners who help govern Theresienstadt. They are Jews, most of them professors or medical doctors from places like Prague, Berlin or Amsterdam. The council oversees such things as the allocation of living quarters, the division of labor, the division of rations, the water supply system and the bogus bank. They are also responsible for compiling the transport lists.

If we refused to leave our barracks, the other prisoners might have taken us for heroes.

But when I see Father and Mother kiss on the lips, I feel sure we are doing the right thing. Besides, I tell myself, had any of the gossiping women in the barracks been given a similar offer, surely they would have packed their satchels and left straightaway for Jagergasse.

The four of us open the door to our room. Though it is dark and stinks of mildew, we all know how lucky we are to have it. A room to ourselves! The artists' studio is two floors up. Our new quarters, allocated by the Council of Elders, are a reward for Father's hard work. He has been working himself to the bone.

While Mother keeps count of who gets soup, and Theo stokes the fires in one of the workshops, and I scrub in the diet kitchen, Father works long days in the artists' studio. Mostly, he tells us, he restores old paintings, ones the Nazis have looted from Jewish homes. Sometimes he draws charts or makes signs.

Though Father's work is less dirty than cleaning latrines or stoking fires, it's far from easy. He cannot make mistakes or waste paper. And he must face the same kinds of humiliation as the rest of us.

Last week, Father made signs for the bathrooms in the Nazis' new mess hall: *herren* and *damen*, the German words for men and women. He told us how he was on a ladder in the mess hall, hanging his signs when two Nazis and their families came in. It was one of the children's birthdays, and the others were carrying gifts.

"It was a strange experience," Father told us on our Sunday visit, "to see those officers with their wives and children, behaving like normal men. But then, one of the women spotted me on the ladder. 'What's that ugly Jew doing here?' she asked, pointing her finger at me. 'Get him out at once or he'll ruin our party!' And I skulked out of the mess hall, like a dog with his tail between his legs."

Father looked crestfallen when he told us the story. For a moment, I wished I could scoop him up in my arms and comfort him. But then he'd turned to me and said, "All that matters is that we are still together." Though my heart was breaking for him, I knew he was right.

Mother pushes open the window at the back of the apartment. It looks out on a pile of rubble. Across the way is the supplies barracks. Not that it has much to offer in the way of supplies. The barracks is stocked with discards from the *Schleuse*. But if someone needs a cane or a piece of rotting wood, this is the place to find it.

Theo runs in circles around the apartment. "Stop!" Mother cries out, grabbing him from behind. "You're making me dizzy." Then she covers his head with kisses. "My Theo," she says, rumpling his hair. "How I've missed you."

The apartment is only one room, but Mother has found a tattered cotton sheet in the supplies barrack, and soon it is hanging across the middle of the room. "This will be your's and Theo's side," she explains. "This will be mine and Father's. That way we can have some privacy."

There is an electric hot plate and a bathroom, though it has no running water. But there are just as many bedbugs and fleas as there were in the barracks. Before bedtime, the four of us work hard to tear the bedbugs' bodies from our blankets. Theo and I crush them on the floor. But now that it is dark, the bugs are back in full force.

I hear the soft murmur of Mother and Father's voices from behind the curtain. "Stupid bugs!" Theo curses. "Goddamn Jew bugs!"

"Stop it, Theo," I tell him. "We need to sleep." How could I have forgotten how annoying Theo is? And to think that he is calling the bugs "Jew bugs"!

"Don't argue," Father says from behind the curtain. "All that matters is that we are still together."

When I wake up the next morning, Theo is gone. I nearly cry out until I hear the familiar sound of his breathing.

Theo has gone to sleep in the bathtub.

"Hardly any bedbugs there," he announces as if he is Christopher Columbus and has discovered some exotic foreign land.

⁓

"Are you upset with me?" I ask Hannelore.

Our faces are pressed against the shop window. One of the streets behind the center square is lined with small stores, though in reality they are more storefronts than actual stores. The grocery store, for example, stocks nothing but mustard. Jars and jars of it line the wooden shelves inside. Who wants to eat mustard without a sausage to dip in it?

But from the outside, to a casual visitor—one who doesn't step inside the stores or climb the barracks to the upper levels where the old people live, looking more like cadavers than human beings—Theresienstadt could pass for an ordinary little town. A bit down on its luck, overcrowded and smelling of sewage and sweat...but still a town.

Hannelore hasn't said anything about the fact that Mother and I no longer live in the barracks.

"I'm not upset," Hannelore says. "I'm glad for you. That's what I told my mother when she said your father is working for the Naz—" Hannelore blushes and covers her mouth with one hand.

"That isn't fair," I say. The air between us feels as if it's been charged by lightning. How dare her mother say something like that? This is the closest Hannelore and I have ever come to an argument. "When you and I scrub cauldrons, we're working for the Nazis too," I tell her.

Hannelore nods. "Of course, you're right. That's what I told my mother."

A moment later Hannelore seems to forget our quarrel. "Look!" she cries out, tapping on the window. "Do you see that black velvet skirt? That one...at the back."

"Yes, I see it."

"I believe it's mine!" Hannelore's voice quivers with excitement. "I wonder how much they want for it."

Hannelore and I walk into the clothing shop. A Czech prisoner sits at a desk, writing in a ledger book. Sometimes it seems to me the inhabitants of Theresienstadt spend more time keeping records of things than doing anything else. I can't see the point of all these records. Father's meticulously drawn charts are also a form of record keeping. He draws charts indicating the cost of maintaining each inmate: four pence a day, up from three pence in 1942; the number of inmates able to work versus those who are too infirm; charts of those who qualify for an extra ration of sugar; charts of those who have been sent on the latest transport.

Father's charts, he explained, are submitted every Friday to the Nazi high command in Berlin. "I don't see much point either, Anneke," he confided to me, "but if it keeps my family alive, I'll happily do it. I'd do anything to ensure your survival," he added, his voice growing husky. "Anything."

When Father said that, mostly I felt comforted. Father would do anything—risk anything—to keep us alive. Surely that means we have a chance of getting through all this. But something about the fierce way Father said, "I'd do anything. Anything," frightens me a little too. I hope Father will never have to hurt anyone else to protect himself—and us.

"It *is* my skirt! I remember the day Mother brought it home for me!" Hannelore says as she lifts the skirt off the rack. "They took it from me at the *Schleuse*."

For a moment, I remember my golden brooch and wonder where it might be and who is wearing it. The daughter of some Nazi officer, no doubt. My pulse quickens. I can imagine her delight on the evening her father brought it home. "It's so delicate," she'd have said, "and twenty-four-karat gold." She'd have gazed at her own reflection in the tiny mirror, just as I'd done when it was mine. Did that girl really believe her father had purchased the brooch for her? Had he perhaps put it in a small velvet box before he'd presented his gift? Or did she suspect the brooch was stolen from another girl? And if she did, did she ever wonder about me, what I was like and what kind of life I lived?

I sigh as I consider the injustice of it all. Here we are in this twisted city, told over and over again that we are the lucky ones, and all because we are the descendants of Abraham and Sarah, some Jews in the desert long ago who meant nothing—absolutely nothing—to me! In fact they cursed me, those people! Isn't it because of them I'm here?

And there goes Hannelore inquiring about the cost of her own velvet skirt. This store is stocked entirely with clothing that was confiscated at the *Schleuse*—pants, skirts, sweaters, coats, boots and shoes. None of it is in very good condition. I don't want to hurt Hannelore's feelings, but I can see the seam of her skirt has begun to fray and the velvet has lost its shine. No, anything of value, including my brooch, would have been sent to the high command offices in Berlin.

Occasionally we are issued ghetto *kronen* for our work. On the bills is a drawing of a coarse-looking Moses carrying tablets. The bills are issued by the Jewish bank in Theresienstadt. They can be spent on mustard or to buy back the clothes that were stolen from us. The whole thing makes me so angry I could spit.

Hannelore doesn't seem to realize the awfulness of it all. She digs into her pocket for her *kronen* and buys the skirt.

"It's lovely," I lie.

When I leave for the soup kitchen the next morning, Franticek Halop is standing at the corner, his hands deep in his pockets. His dark curls are so greasy they stick to his scalp. Still, the sight of him makes something catch in my throat.

Though we have never spoken, I know he's noticed me, perhaps because there are not many blue-eyed fair-haired girls in Theresienstadt. Most of the girls here have dark eyes and hair like Hannelore. I've caught Franticek eyeing me when he is out with his group of friends, and I know he's seen me blush.

I also know about the girlfriend. She is an older woman with two small children. I've heard she even has a

husband in one of the men's barracks. In Theresienstadt,
things like that don't matter much. I've seen Franticek
and the girlfriend—she has dark hair that frames her
face, and breasts like apples—sneak into one of the
cubbyholes at the central kitchen on a Sunday afternoon.
We all know what the cubbyholes are for. Later that day,
I saw the girlfriend standing in line for soup with her
two children, her cheeks flushed, her hair mussed up.
I burned with jealousy.

Now here is Franticek standing at the corner,
grinning as he sees me approach. His smile, lopsided,
reminds me of a little boy's. Could he be waiting for me?
I turn around to see if there is a prettier girl behind me,
one with rounder breasts or wider hips, maybe even the
girlfriend. But no, there are only old people, hurrying to
their work.

Franticek holds out his hand when I pass.

And to my own surprise, I take it.

What will Hannelore say when I tell her?

Franticek's hand feels warm and dry. When he
squeezes my fingers, I feel my knees grow weak. The
place where my thighs meet tingles in a way I've never
felt before. I would like to say something, but for once,
I have no words. No stories to tell.

All I want to do is concentrate on the feeling of my
hand in his. I've never felt such pleasure, not even when,
after a dance at the Amsterdam Lyceum, I kissed Johan
with an open mouth. We were both embarrassed afterward, and we never did it again.

Franticek stops in front of the diet kitchen. So he knows where I work! Surely that means he cares for me.

"What's your name?" he asks in a velvety voice.

"Anneke," I stammer.

"I'm Franticek."

"I know."

I shouldn't have said that. Now he'll think I like him. But it is too late to take it back. Franticek smiles.

Later that morning, when I'm back in the diet kitchen, I scrub with an energy I never knew I was capable of.

Six

"Why can't *you* do portraits?" I ask Father.

It is a chilly Sunday in October, and I rub my hands together to keep them warm. If our apartment is this cold now, what will it be like in February?

Father looks pained. "I do cartoons," he says, a little crossly. His face has grown even thinner. "The public seems to appreciate my work."

"But why not *portraits*?" I insist.

"Your father is a great cartoonist," Mother interrupts. She is dusting. Not that there is much to dust—only our plywood table and a bench that lurches to one side. If I sit down at the wrong end, I feel like I am on a seesaw. But dusting seems to lift Mother's spirits. Sometimes, I catch her humming while she dusts, and I wonder if, for a few minutes at least, she is back in our sunny parlor in Broek.

Petr Kien has asked whether he might do my portrait. He is one of my father's favorite colleagues in the studio. "A real prodigy, especially for such a young man. He studied with Willi Nowak in Prague," I heard Father tell Mother.

Petr Kien is much younger than Father. He is tall with a long pale face. A poet's face, which makes sense, since he also occasionally writes poems. Like us, he has his own quarters, which he shares with his wife and her parents.

Today he's come to our room to do the portrait. He has set up a makeshift easel, fashioned out of planks he found in the supplies barracks. As with everything else, the Nazis keep careful count of the art supplies. At the end of their workday, Father and the other painters in his studio have to return the paint jars to their locked cabinet, and the supervisor records the number of sheets of cardboard used that day.

But artists in Theresienstadt have ways of getting hold of supplies for their own personal use. A discarded drawing sometimes still has a fresh unused side. With care, a paintbrush and bottle of ink can be smuggled out in a pocket. And the right size bits of charred wood make a passable charcoal.

Though Petr Kien is trained as an oil painter, he uses charcoal to sketch me. I'm sitting on the edge of Father and Mother's mattress. "Look toward the door," he tells me. I do exactly as he says.

Father is standing behind Petr Kien. Mother and Petr Kien's wife, who's come along to keep her husband company and visit with Mother, are watching too. I'm hungry, but I feel a little swelling in my belly. I think it's pride. A talented artist has asked to sketch me. Perhaps I'm more beautiful than I realized!

"She has such lovely blond ringlets," Petr Kien says as he begins sketching, his fingertips already black from the coal.

You see? So he admires my hair. But compliments embarrass me. "I get my hair from Father," I say. I try not to laugh because I don't want to ruin the pose.

But everyone else laughs. Father's head is as bald as an egg.

I am not accustomed to sitting still. Nor am I accustomed to so much attention. But I have to admit that it is rather nice. "She's quite unusual-looking," says Frau Kien.

Mother serves her weak tea in one of the four enamel cups we brought from Holland and which we were allowed to keep. For a moment, I think of the serviettes Mother embroidered by hand which she liked to use at home when her lady friends visited.

Father leans down so he can be even closer to Petr Kien. From behind his glasses, Father's eyes dart between the cardboard and me. "It's already an excellent likeness, Kien," he says.

Petr Kien blushes but makes no reply. Instead he focuses on the sketch—and me. Again, I get the feeling that I must be someone quite special. I try not to move, but then the tip of my nose gets itchy, and I have to scratch it. I do so quickly, hoping Father will not notice. For Father, art is the most important thing. More important by far than itchy noses.

Petr Kien rubs at the drawing. Perhaps he wants to create a shady spot. He purses his lips while he works, as if that will help him get my likeness right. From where I'm sitting, I can hear the steady sound of his breathing.

Another of Mother's friends comes knocking at the door. It is Countess Bratovska. One of the few Russians in the camp, her husband was a Russian count. And even as she walks into our tiny dark apartment, the countess carries herself like royalty. It doesn't take much imagination to picture her wearing an ermine stole, with emeralds around her neck. And a tiara. A diamond tiara.

I imagine the fancy dress balls she and her husband must have attended together. I can see her stepping out of their carriage, one footman standing by to take her hand, another making sure the train of her dress does not get wet from the snow. I've heard that in St. Petersburg, where Countess Bratovska and her husband lived, there are mountains of snow in winter.

I try to hold my head a little higher.

Mother hurriedly prepares more tea. "I'm so sorry I have nothing to offer you with it. But I do have one special treat—there's sugar," she says proudly. "Jo, can you get it for me?"

Father gets up from his spot behind Petr Kien and reaches for the shelf over the table. It is empty, except for Mother's porcelain sugar bowl. Inside are exactly four lumps of sugar. I know because I've counted them. Sugar is a special treat. Father earned these lumps in exchange for a drawing.

Ghetto *kronen* are not the only form of currency in Theresienstadt. There are also cigarettes and paintings. Two cigarettes can buy you a potato. But if you are caught with them, cigarettes can also cost you your life. It amazes me that though we are all starving, there are prisoners who would forego food in favor of a smoke. I vow that if I survive, I will never ever take up the vile habit.

Petr Kien is not charging us for the sketch he's making today. But he could if he wanted to. In the camp, sketches and paintings are even more valuable than cigarettes, especially if the artwork is produced by someone famous, like Petr Kien or Father. And while forgoing food for two cigarettes strikes me as ludicrous, sacrificing food for art makes a certain sense. I am, after all, an artist's daughter. Haven't I played in Father's studio while he made his magic and watched over his shoulder in amazement as he turned simple lines into little people and cows and dogs? No, Father does not do portraits. But the people he paints are as full of life as Petr Kien's.

When I suck on a lump of sugar, I can forget for a moment how hungry I am or how sore my throat is. Father's friend, Dr. Hayek, says it's tonsillitis. But since there's no medicine for prisoners, I've had to get used to the pain.

"I prefer my tea black," Countess Bratovska says.

I thought Theo was too busy playing in the corner to pay attention to the adults' conversation. But I am wrong because now he sighs with relief. He will still have his lump of sugar.

Mother glares at him.

Father is peering down at the countess's wrist. What has he seen and why does he look so worried? And then, suddenly, I see it too: a louse—shiny, black and ready to bite.

Father clears his throat. "Your royal h...highness," he stammers. "There seems to be a...a louse crawling up your sleeve. If you will permit..."

The countess barely blinks. "Certainly," she says.

Father's aim is good. He slaps once, loudly, and the louse is dead. It falls to the floor, and a moment later, Mother sweeps it up.

"Are you sure you wouldn't like a lump of sugar in your tea?" Father asks the countess.

Petr Kien never looks up from his work until at last he puts down his charcoal. "Come and tell me what you think, Anneke," he says.

All the adults crowd around the sketch, making impressed-sounding noises. "Such a talent and in such a young man," the countess gushes.

My legs feel stiff from sitting for so long. The adults clear a path for me. They are eager to see my reaction.

Of course I'm curious. I haven't seen my own reflection—except in a dirty window—since I came to Theresienstadt. But when I see the girl that Petr Kien has sketched, I back away. Where is the smiling Dutch girl with the round face?

The girl Petr Kien has captured is a stranger to me. Her face is thin and anxious, pasty-looking. Her chin is pointy, her cheeks are hollow and her hair is stringy. There are dark circles under her eyes. Only the eyes themselves are vaguely familiar.

"What do you think of yourself, Anneke, dear?" the countess asks.

"It's—it's good," I say, nearly choking on the words.

Father pats Petr Kien's shoulder. "You have a remarkable talent, Kien," Father says. I know that means the likeness must resemble me. If I cry, they'll think I am ungrateful. So I fight back the tears. Whatever good looks I once possessed are lost. It's one more thing the Nazis have robbed me of.

⁖⊶

The word "transport" spreads like fire through Theresienstadt. Since mid-morning no one has spoken of anything else. I notice the lines on Frau Davidels' forehead as she talks to a prisoner who mops floors in the diet kitchen. She lowers her voice, but I can still make out the dreaded word.

Through the window, I can see a group of old people gathered outside, clinging to each other, their eyes full of fear. "Do you think our time is up?" I hear an old woman cry out.

Though we have no telephones or newspapers, news travels quickly through Theresienstadt. And though the adults do their best to prevent us from learning the worst, in the end, there are few secrets in the camp.

The rumors about the transport begin when a Nazi official in a smart wool coat is spotted stepping out of a limousine in front of the commandant's headquarters. He is flanked by two more Nazis, and when the three of them march up the stairs, Commandant Rahm himself comes to meet them. We all hate Rahm, an ill-tempered man with veiny cheeks and angry eyes set too close together.

"They say Rahm—that bastard—looked as if he might pee himself meeting the great Adolf Eichmann," one woman in the diet kitchen tells Frau Davidels. On an ordinary day, the thought of the commandant peeing in his pants would make me cry with laughter. But this is no ordinary day.

An hour later, Eichmann and his henchmen emerge from Rahm's headquarters. Eichmann is upset. There is mud on the bottom of his coat. One of the henchmen goes to fetch some soapy water; then he kneels down on the steps to wipe the coat clean. Once that is done, Eichmann claps his hands and steps back inside the limousine. People who see the car drive off say Eichmann, who sits in the backseat, keeps his eyes on the road in front of him. "He'd already forgotten about the lot of us," they say.

"Forgotten?" someone cries out. "You can't forget people you never noticed in the first place. To the Nazis, we're less than nothing."

Within a quarter of an hour, the members of the Council of Elders are summoned to Rahm's headquarters. Their faces are ashen, their shoulders stooped as they enter the building. They know they have a grim task ahead: to supply the names of a thousand inmates who will leave on the next transport. In two days' time.

I hate the members of the Council of Elders. When I pass one of them on the street, I look away. "They're almost as bad as the Nazis," I tell Father. "All they care about is keeping their own names off the transport lists."

Father disagrees. He argues that if it weren't for the council, the Nazis might liquidate Theresienstadt. "We need to have compassion for the council members," he says. "Imagine having to do what's been asked of them."

Hours pass, and people keep careful watch over Rahm's headquarters. But there is no sign of the council. That confirms everyone's worst suspicion: Work on the latest list has already begun.

For the Nazis, the transports are a way to clean up Theresienstadt, no different from Mother's dusting. Theresienstadt is overcrowded, throbbing with Jews. With every new trainload that arrives at Buhosovice, the fate of the camp becomes clear: There will be more transports.

And so for the next two days, we hold our breath. We go to work, we line up for soup, but we think of nothing other than Wednesday's transport. At the end of the day, we walk into our barracks or our rooms, scanning our mattresses for the thin strip of paper which means our name is on the list.

Hannelore and I barely say a word as we walk back from the diet kitchen. We hear terrible weeping coming from one of the men's barracks. But this time, we don't try to listen in or watch. No, we know exactly what this weeping means.

"I'll see you tomorrow," I say, squeezing Hannelore's hand when I leave her at the women's barracks. When we peer in together, my heart beats double-time. But there is no strip of paper on her mattress or her mother's. For now they've been spared.

.:☞

The next morning, the skin around Hannelore's eyes is pink and puffy.

"What's wrong?" I ask, reaching for her hand.

"My Uncle Fritz..." She can barely get the words out.

I gasp. "Perhaps there's still some way..."

It is sometimes possible to get a name removed from the transport list. This explains why there is already a long line of people shuffling outside Commandant Rahm's office. Since yesterday afternoon, they've been waiting for an audience with the head of the Council of Elders. If a strong enough case can be made, you or whomever you are petitioning for might be spared.

Though everyone knows that if a name is dropped from the list, another will have to be added.

Then there are the horror stories about what has happened to some of the prisoners who petitioned directly to the Nazis. Herr Adler, who was in charge of Father's studio, was devastated when he learned that the names of three of his artists had been added, at the last moment, to a transport list. Adler rushed to the train and pleaded with one of the Nazi guards. "Please, I beg of you. You have three of my workers. Talented, hard-working men from my studio. Their names are…" The Nazi grabbed Adler by his collar and threw him onto the train. "If you're so eager to be reunited with your comrades," he snarled, "go join them now."

Adler didn't even have a chance to say good-bye to his wife and children.

And though it is a terrible thought, I knew we benefited from what happened to Adler. The Council of Elders promoted Father to chief of the studio, and because of that, we'd been able to move to our quarters on Jagergasse.

When Father was first offered the new position, he told us he had tried to decline. "Look what happened to Adler!" Father had told Dr. Epstein, the head of the Council of Elders.

But Epstein shook his head. "Van Raalte," he said in a tired voice, "don't you see? You haven't any choice."

All this is one more bitter truth about life in Theresienstadt: One person's agony often means someone else's gain. And though I am sorry to see others suffer, another part of me—a bigger part— is relieved it isn't me. I know it's awful, but that's how it is.

Some other family, perhaps even the Adlers, had lived in our room on Jagergasse before us. They left the rickety plywood table behind. But I didn't want to think about them, or where they might be now. No, I was just glad I was out of the barracks, away from the other women's moans and shouting in the middle of the night.

"But your uncle is an architect," I say to Hannelore while we are scrubbing our cauldrons. Today, with so much tension in the air, Frau Davidels forgets to chide us for talking, even when a Nazi officer drops into the diet kitchen and sniffs at the contents of one of the cauldrons. "Isn't your uncle on the prominent list?"

Hannelore sniffles. "Uncle Fritz's health has been so poor, what with his asthma and arthritis, that lately he hasn't been strong enough to work."

So, Hannelore's uncle has been removed from the list of prominent prisoners. I don't say what I am thinking: Everyone whose name is on the list can protect up to four family members. Does that mean Hannelore and her mother are no longer protected? My throat tightens and for a moment, I have trouble breathing. Hannelore has become my closest friend, closer than any friend I've ever had, and I can't imagine a day in Theresienstadt without her.

We have made plans for after the war. We'll corre-
spond and visit each other during school holidays. When
we have children, they will be close friends. If one day,
I have a son, and Hannelore has a daughter, they'll fall
in love and marry. What a wedding it will be!

Hannelore laughs when I tell her this. Then she
wags her finger in the air. "If there is an after the war,"
Hannelore says.

And now, I wonder, if indeed there will be an after
the war for Hannelore and her mother, and for me
and my family. If names can be taken off the protected
list, what guarantee is there that Father's name will
remain on it?

·⁖ᴏ~

By Tuesday evening, the mood changes. I'd seen it
happen before, always the night before a transport. "For
all we know," Countess Bratovska tells Mother and me
when we are lining up for soup, "those people leaving
tomorrow are going to a better place, one that's less
crowded and where they'll have better dinners than this
miserable soup."

"There's not even a scrap of meat in it tonight,"
says a man standing closer to the front of the line.

"Let's hope for those poor souls on tomorrow's train
that you're right," Mother whispers to the countess.

A woman wearing a skirt made of rags that have been
sewn together elbows the countess. "With a thousand

fewer people in the camp tomorrow, there may be meat in tomorrow's soup." Her eyes gleam as she speaks.

··◌⌒

Mother hands me a small bar of gray soap and a pile of our filthy clothes. "But it isn't laundry day," I protest. Because of the shortage of clean water, we are only permitted to wash clothes every six weeks—and then only up to four kilograms of laundry—which doesn't amount to much when you consider there are four of us.

"Father sold a sketch to one of the women at the washing fountain. In return, she's letting us do an extra wash. Go quickly to the fountain and see how much of this you can get done. I'd do it myself, but your father isn't feeling well."

My stomach turns. "He isn't?"

Mother pushes me toward the door. "Go," she says. "He'll be fine."

The bundle Mother has given me is large and hard to carry. I can barely see over it and items of clothing—a tattered undershirt, an old sock—keep falling off. Soon I'm sweaty from trying to keep the bundle together. The insides of my elbows ache.

Franticek is at the corner. I have no free hand to wipe the sweat off my face, so I try brushing it against the pile of clothes. The stink of sweat burns my nostrils. Now my face will smell too. And I can feel rings of sweat forming under my armpits. If I keep my arms close to my chest, Franticek may not notice.

I feel ashamed of the soiled clothing I am carrying. What if he sees my underpants? What will he think of me then? If only I had a free hand for him to hold!

But Franticek laughs. "Imagine my good fortune, running into you," he says, playing with the piece of black leather he wears around his neck.

"Do you believe in luck?" I ask him, suddenly feeling bolder than usual.

"A little," he says, casting his dark eyes down to the cobblestone street. "But we make our own luck. That's why sometimes I wait for you here at night."

"You do?" I feel myself blush.

Franticek follows me to the fountain. At first I refuse his offer to help me wash the dirty laundry, but when he insists, I give him a pair of Theo's socks. The socks, it seems, have more holes than wool in them. "You'd better have a strong nose," I warn him.

When Franticek laughs, his dark eyes light up. As he scrubs the socks, I think how Franticek is not only handsome, but kind.

"Anneke," he says, "I need to tell you about my feelings for you."

I can practically feel my heart skip a beat. Just the way they say it happens in storybooks. Only usually the girl isn't washing underwear, rubbing the soap so hard the skin on her knuckles breaks. And usually the boy doesn't go off with someone else into cubbyholes.

No, I tell myself, this is wrong. All wrong.

"What about your lady friend?" I ask, my voice suddenly growing shrill. "The one with the two children?"

This time, Franticek blushes. Does he really think I've never seen them together?

"I don't love her," he says, his dark eyes on mine.

He doesn't love her? That only makes things worse! If he doesn't love her, why does he take her to the cubby-holes? I look Franticek straight in the eye. "I've seen the two of you go off together…on Sunday afternoons. And doesn't she have a husband?" I pick at the skin around my fingernail. I've said too much. Now Franticek will know for sure that I've been watching him.

Franticek sucks in his breath and meets my gaze. "What she and I do together," he says, "are just animal things."

"Animal things?" I say as I turn back to my scrubbing. I feel hot tears prick at the corners of my eyes. Animal things? How can he say something so rude? I'm no animal, I'm a human girl. I won't let him speak to me like this.

"Go away," I mutter, without looking up. "Just go away."

As I scrub, I keep my eyes on his feet. He is wearing a pair of scuffed gray boots. The boots don't move an inch. Franticek isn't going away. I could insist, but I don't. I think of Franticek's dark hair and eyes. And though I shouldn't, I think of his calloused hands running across my body, touching my face, my neck, my arms. I know it's very very wrong, but I can't help wondering what it would be like to be in one of the cubbyholes with Franticek. For a moment, a wave of guilty pleasure washes over me.

There are holes at the big toes of both of Franticek's boots. Underneath, I can see a flash of worn red socks. The boots are obviously too small. And suddenly, my feelings change and I am sorry for Franticek with his too-small boots and his worn red socks. Who am I to judge him?

Franticek must feel the change in me, because when he speaks again, his voice is calm. "You have to understand," he says, "I'm not proud of it, but a person...well, a person has to survive. And in a place like this," he lifts his eyes toward the tall gray ramparts that surround us, blocking our view of the outside world, "sometimes a person has to take what he can get. Just to feel alive."

My head is reeling. Certainly this business about animal things is all wrong. Yet what Franticek says makes a kind of sense. And another part of me is simply curious. What are these animal things exactly, and do they have anything to do with how I feel when Franticek holds my hand: the tingling sensations, the ones that start low in my belly and create a heat that courses through my whole body?

I scrub even harder now. So hard the soap flies out of my hands and into the fountain.

If I don't get it back quickly, it will dissolve. Then what will Mother say?

Franticek reaches into the fountain and retrieves my piece of soap from the gray water. The ends of his dark eyelashes are wet. "Here," he says, smiling as his hand touches mine and he gives me the soap. There it is again, the tingling feeling. Only it's even stronger this time. So strong, I can feel it in the soles of my feet.

Franticek kneels down on one knee. "Anneke," he says, "I love you."

I laugh. Franticek looks as if I've given him a smack. "You don't even know me," I tell him.

"You're wrong."

"How could you know me?" I ask him, laying the soap on the edge of the fountain.

"You can know a person from looking in her eyes and from the sound of her laughter. I've heard you laugh, Anneke. With your friend from the diet kitchen."

I look into Franticek's dark eyes. Perhaps he is right. Perhaps I know him too. I've looked into his eyes, and I have heard his throaty laugh. He has even helped me wash my brother's socks.

"I want to give you this." Franticek loosens the thin strip of leather from around his neck. "It isn't much. But it's all I have to give."

"No," I protest, "I can't take it." In the ordinary world, the piece of leather Franticek is offering me has little value. But in the camp, it can be used for a shoe-lace. Shoelaces that aren't frayed or torn to bits are in great demand in Theresienstadt.

"I want you to have it," Franticek insists. "So you'll always remember me."

"Remember you?" What does he mean by that? "Franticek," I say, my voice breaking, "you're not..."

Franticek's eyes drop to his boots. I get up from my spot and move toward him, so close I can reach my arms around his back. He is so thin I can feel his bones. My arms and legs are trembling. Franticek trembles too. I hold him a little closer.

He ties the leather strip around my neck, careful not to let it catch in my curls. The little hairs on the back of my neck stand up when I feel his touch.

When Franticek brings his lips to mine, I don't object.

Franticek's lips are rough chapped, but for some reason I can't quite understand, his mouth tastes sweet. Sweet and somehow earthy at the same time. I am thinking too much. Stop all this thinking, I tell myself, as I part my lips and let myself sink into the kiss.

Franticek is right. People need to take what they can. People need to feel alive. This kiss is what I need to take to feel alive. When it finally ends, and Franticek brushes one finger against my lips, I can feel tears pricking at the corners of my eyes. Franticek wipes them away. Then he brings his finger to his mouth and tastes my tears.

Neither of us says a word as Franticek walks me back to Jagergasse. I've wrung out the laundry as best I can, and Franticek is carrying some of it. The leather strip feels good against my neck. I'll never take it off. Never.

We are on Jagergasse now. Franticek kisses my fore-head once, lightly. "Always remember," he says, his voice hoarse. "Promise me."

"I promise." The tears are coming back. How can all this be happening? How can Franticek tell me he loves me and then be going away? Because of course that's what it all means—the things he's said, the leather neck-lace. Franticek is leaving on tomorrow's transport.

I cling to him. I don't care if Father or Mother or Theo sees us through the window.

But it is Frau Davidels who finds us. "Anneke," she says, her voice as brisk and businesslike as it is in the diet kitchen when one of the Nazi supervisors is around.

"Come quickly." She tugs on my elbow. "Your father has been taken to the infirmary. They think it's diphtheria."

Seven

"Why can't *I* go see Father?" Theo asks. He's lost all his baby fat in Theresienstadt and grown a little taller, but he is still a nuisance.

"You're too young," I tell him.

"You're too ugly, but they let *you* visit him."

"Come on, Theo," I say. I am doing my best to ignore the nasty thing he just said.

Frau Davidels has offered to watch Theo while I join Mother at the infirmary. "It's good for me to be around a little boy again," Frau Davidels told me, her eyes a little misty. I knew she was thinking about the son she'd lost.

Father has been in the infirmary for over a week, since the night before Franticek left on the transport. I tug on the leather necklace he gave me. It makes me feel a little better to know his fingers touched it. How I miss him, and how I hope he is still alive. It hurts too much to consider any other possibility, and when I do, my whole body goes icy cold. What if someone has hurt Franticek? What if he is already buried in some pit? No, no, I tell myself, that cannot be. Besides, I'm convinced that without Franticek, my world would end. And because I woke up this morning, Franticek must still be alive, mustn't he?

Since Franticek's departure, I've begun doing something I never did before, and never imagined myself doing. I've begun to pray. I didn't really know how it was done, since I'd never been to synagogue, and so I made it up. As if praying was one of my stories.

I know Father wouldn't approve. He thinks religion is a form of superstition; hocus-pocus, he calls it. Only right now, I need some hocus-pocus, something to give me hope that Franticek is still alive.

I don't know what else to do or who else to ask for help. So every night, before I crawl onto my mattress, I drop to my knees and pray to God. "Please Lord," I tell Him, "I understand that there are many people who need you during these dark days. But please, if you could consider my requests. There are only two. Could you look after Franticek? Help him stay strong and don't let him suffer too much. And please, please could you also restore Father's health so that we can be together again?"

The praying hurts my knees because of the wood floors in our apartment, but at least it makes me feel like I am doing something. I hope God, if He really exists, won't be upset with me for only turning to him now, when things are so bleak. But I have a feeling He will understand my predicament.

Perhaps Countess Bratovska is right. Perhaps Franticek has been sent to a place where there are fewer people and larger rations. He is young and strong, so perhaps he is helping build a new camp in the east. Yes, I like to picture him chopping wood or laying stone, the muscles in his shoulders rippling as he works. The thought of anything else—that the rumors we've heard of Jews being tortured and killed in death camps might be true—is too terrible to contemplate.

As I enter the infirmary, I nearly run into a little boy with a very pale face. He is carrying something, coddling it like it is a tiny baby.

"What have you got there?" I ask him.

His dark eyes light up. "An egg."

"An egg?" I am impressed. I haven't seen an egg since we came to Theresienstadt. I'm sure the Nazi officers get to eat them for breakfast, but not us prisoners. How has this child managed to get an egg?

"I have TBC," he tells me. It's the abbreviation we prisoners use for tuberculosis. "So tonight I got an egg with my dinner. It's hardboiled." He opens his hands to show it to me. It's a brown egg—a big one. For a moment, I remember the rich taste of egg yolk and the way it sometimes dripped across my plate, leaving a yellow trail. "Can you believe my good luck?" the boy asks.

"You are very lucky," I tell him. As I open the door to Father's room, I hear the little boy's cough, dry and ragged, echo down the hallway. Tuberculosis is a terrible disease. I wonder how much time the boy has left.

Mother is sitting by Father's bedside. His eyes are closed, but his breathing is steady. I lean down to kiss Father's forehead. It feels hot and clammy.

"It's best not to get too close," Mother whispers.

I nod, and she notices me wince when I swallow.

"How is your throat today?" she asks.

"I'm fine," I tell her. But I am not fine. My throat hurts almost all the time, but I don't want to give Mother any more to worry about.

While Father is in the infirmary, he is getting reduced rations, and if he is going to recover, he needs his strength. Thank goodness for Frau Davidels' potatoes. And for Petr Kien, who brought Father a chunk of black bread the other night.

I make myself a spot at the end of Father's cot.

"Anneke," Mother whispers. "There's something we need to discuss." I knew it would only be a matter of time before Mother asked about Franticek. She and Frau Davidels have become good friends, and Frau Davidels saw Franticek and me together...the night we kissed. That wonderful, terrible night.

"Else told me about you and the boy," Mother says. For the first time, I notice that the hair at her temples is streaked with gray. Mother's beautiful thick auburn hair that she was always so proud of. And she's not even forty.

I don't want to talk to Mother about Franticek. I want to keep Franticek to myself, like a kind of treasure that is just mine.

She reaches for my hand and squeezes it the way she used to when we walked together in Broek. "Anneke, you're growing up and there are things you need to know...about men and women." Mother's cheeks redden, but she keeps talking. "Else told me that you and the boy were kissing. Passionately."

The tears sting at my eyes as I remember the feeling of Franticek's lips on mine and how sweet he tasted. "He's gone," I tell my mother, blurting out the words. "On the last transport."

For a brief moment, the lines on Mother's forehead seem to disappear. Is she relieved? The thought fills me with anger. How can she be so selfish? But then Mother's face changes again, and she gets up from her seat to take me in her arms. "Anneke," she says, her voice thick with tears, "my dear, dear Anneke."

Eight

The lights wake us before the noise. Search beams shine in through our window, making wide white arcs against the wall. Where am I? I wonder for a moment. In Broek? On holiday in Paris with Father and Mother and Theo? But when I look up at the gray wood planks on the ceiling I know exactly where I am. My mouth tastes sour. My stomach grumbles from hunger.

"What's going on?" Theo calls from the bathtub.

Mother is up now too. She is opening the curtain that separates our "rooms," a bewildered look on her face.

The light hurts my eyes. When I moan, Mother gives me a sharp look. "Anneke!" she says.

"Everyone outside! Everyone outside immediately! *Raus!*" an angry voice crackles over a loudspeaker and then fades into the darkness. The sound is coming from a car that is being driven around the camp. Soon, it is back again. "*Raus! Raus!*" Now there is honking.

Because, by now, we are accustomed to following orders, the three of us put on our tattered outer clothing, pull on whatever is left of our boots and rush out the door.

I look longingly at my mattress on the floor. The air is cold and harsh.

There isn't time to wonder why the whole camp is being forced out of bed at two in the morning. And in the rain, no less! Besides, there is no point in wondering, just as there is no point in questioning anything the Nazis do.

I watch as Mother reaches for the shelf and slips the four sugar cubes into her pocket. "Don't forget your cap," she tells Theo. "Anneke, are you wearing your sweater?"

"I hate that cap," Theo says. "The material feels scratchy."

"Just wear it."

By the time we get outside, Jagergasse is swarming with people. I spot Petr Kien with his arm around his wife. His in-laws are stumbling behind them. I am too sleepy to greet them. It doesn't take long before the rain soaks through my jacket. I can tell that, unless it lets up soon, it will soak through the rest of my clothes. Because it's dark and difficult to see where I am going, I step into a puddle. Now my socks are sopping wet too. The smell of wet wool fills my nostrils and makes me feel even colder and more unhappy.

"What do you suppose they have planned for us?" an old man asks. No one answers because no one knows, and we are too sleepy to speculate.

The crackling voice in the car is back again. "To the exercise field at the Buhosovice Basin! Everyone to the exercise field! This is a census count," it announces. *Honk! Honk!*

The exercise field is a valley on the edge of the camp, between the road and the river.

"A census count? In the middle of the night? It makes no sense," I mutter to Mother as we join the huge throng of prisoners that looks like a black snake slithering in the dark toward the field. The air is damp and heavy. The rain is getting stronger, pelting down against our faces.

Mother takes Theo's arm, and I know to stay close. "Things stopped making sense a long time ago," she says.

The one good thing about the cold and the rain is that they help wake us up. But my throat throbs, and I wish I had thicker socks. Thicker dry socks.

"What about Father?" Theo asks. "Do you think they'll make him come to be counted too?"

For a moment, Mother shuts her eyes. When she speaks, her voice is tight. "Let's hope not."

Every street we pass is full of prisoners. From a distance, they look like ants. When I get closer I can see them: young and old, all pale and thin, most of them yawning or wiping the sleep from their eyes. Sleep—if we are lucky enough to be able to ignore the bedbugs and lice and doze off for a few hours—is our only escape in Theresienstadt.

I've never seen such a crowd of people as I do once we reach the field. They are milling in circles inside other circles, muttering about having been awakened in the middle of the night and speculating about how long a census count can possibly take.

"Hours! Don't you see how many of us there are? We're going to be here for days," I hear a man with a heavy Czech accent say.

"If they don't kill us first," adds his neighbor.

When I shiver, it isn't just from the cold seeping through my clothes the way the rain has already done.

Somehow, even in the mass of bodies, Frau Davidels manages to find us. She kisses Mother on the cheek. "Have you heard any news of the infirmary?" I hear Mother ask. Even in the dark, I can see the little lines around Mother's mouth; they look like a kind of roadmap.

I push Theo away so I can hear better. He kicks me in the shin.

"They haven't forced them out of the infirmary," Frau Davidels says. "Your Jo should be able to continue resting."

When Mother smiles her old smile, I nearly forget the throbbing in my throat—and the new pain in my shin.

.·☙~

The Nazis make us form rows of five, then twenty rows of five to make a hundred. This will make us easier to count. Theo and I huddle between Mother and Frau Davidels. At least the other bodies so close help warm us a little. It isn't just the November chill that's hard to bear, there is also the damp. The rain keeps getting heavier.

It's coming down at an angle now, beating down against our faces. Around me, people's feet make squishing sounds inside their boots. And soon, the tiredness that disappeared temporarily when I was roused from my sleep, returns. If only I could rest, even for a few minutes.

After two hours of standing and waiting, I feel as if I might keel over. When I lean on Mother's arm, she nearly topples over. She, too, is having trouble staying upright. The cold is making goose bumps on her arm.

"Don't horses sleep standing up?" I ask her.

Theo rubs his eyes. "I wish I was a horse."

Poor Theo. He looks so small and thin and tired. I can almost forgive him for kicking me. "I wish you were a horse," I tell him. "A golden palomino. Then you could give me a ride. Giddee up!" I say, and I pretend to be cracking a whip. Perhaps my story will distract him.

Theo laughs and makes a whinnying sound. "Tell me more about your palomino," he says.

But a Nazi soldier hears Theo's laughter. "Shut up, you useless stinking Jews!" the soldier barks.

Theo freezes in his spot. I am so used to their insults, I don't flinch.

"Twenty-five thousand, four hundred." There are three more Nazis: the one who is counting and two others with clipboards, who are recording information.

I turn to look behind us. The rows extend so far I can't see all the way to the end. I knew the camp was full, but to see so many prisoners all together makes my breath catch in my throat. To think there could be so much misery in one small place!

"I have to pee," I tell Mother.

She sighs. "Can you hold it in?"

"I'll try."

But I have already been holding it in. When I can't manage any longer, I know I have to find a latrine. Only there aren't any on the field. I press my thighs together to make the discomfort go away. But the cold air and the rain only increase my sense of urgency.

Mother notices. "People are going there," she says, pointing to her right. "Shall I come with you?"

I shake my head no.

Mother is right. In the direction she has pointed I see people squatting on the muddy ground as they relieve themselves. I cringe at the sight of them. What have the Nazis reduced us to?

I rush to join the group. When I pull down my pants, the cold air shoots up against my naked buttocks. For the first time, I'm grateful Franticek is no longer in Theresienstadt. If he could see me now, I think, he might never want to kiss me again.

The pee I make takes so long I think it will never end. I lower my face and let my cheeks warm up a little in the steam my pee produces as it hits the cold earth. There is nothing I detest more than the latrines at Theresienstadt, yet now I long for them and for the little squares of magazine we use for toilet paper.

※

"Can't we go home yet?" Theo asks.

"Soon," Mother tells him.

But Mother is wrong. Just when we think the Nazis have finished their count, we learn they have decided to start all over again. Their numbers have not tallied. "Why couldn't they get it right the first time?" people wonder out loud.

"Shh," a voice says. "Don't let them hear you say that."

"It's not about the count," someone else calls out, "it's about torturing us."

Theo leans heavily against my side. Had he been better fed in Theresienstadt, he might be taller than me by now.

I push Theo away. He's hurting me, leaning on me this way. "Stop it," I mutter.

I can't let out my anger against the Nazis—for keeping us here in the camp, and now for forcing us to line up and be counted like animals—but at least I can be angry with Theo.

Just when I think I can't take the waiting and the damp cold any longer, Mother hands me a lump of sugar.

There is one for each of us, and one left over for Frau Davidels. Now I have to make a decision: whether to bite down on the lump or let it dissolve on my tongue. Biting down will be best flavor-wise, but in the end, I decide to let it dissolve on my tongue. The taste will be less intense, but the pleasure will last longer.

Soon the sweetness begins to fill my mouth, making its way to the back of my throat. Anything good, any bit of pleasure, makes me think of Franticek. "People have to take what they can get," he told me.

I can hear Theo crunch down on his lump of sugar.

"You're wasting it," I tell him.

Theo's eyes are closed, but at least he's stopped hanging on me. The sugar gives him a little energy, as it does to me. My body feels as if it's coming back to life. But the feeling doesn't last long. And when I grow tired again, I am even more tired than before.

Someone in front of us moans. About two hundred meters ahead, a woman collapses. Her neighbors try to pull her to her feet. But they don't get to her in time. The entire field seems to grow suddenly still as a Nazi soldier rushes toward the fallen woman, his hand on the pistol in his pocket. The rest of us watch in horror as he takes out his gun, cocks it and shoots the woman in the head.

The sound of the shot rings through the air even after blood begins to seep from her ear. No one dares cry out for fear we might be next.

Just when I think things cannot get any worse, I hear a loud whirring in the air. "German airplanes!" someone shouts. "Bombers!"

Bombers? Why would the Nazis send bombers now?

We crouch together on the wet ground, crying and shaking. The fear eats at my insides like a parasite, hollowing me out until it feels as if there is nothing left of me. Except pure fear. Pure cold fear.

The airplanes dip down over the field like hawks swooping in on their prey. One comes so close I can feel the wind of its wings and hear the screws on the wings rattle. The noise of the engines is almost too much to bear. A woman near me screams, but I can't hear her over the engines. I can only see her mouth open in terror.

I try to block the sound by covering my ears. But it doesn't help. Surely, they are going to kill us. Is this, I wonder, how my life will end? Just like that—without any final words or ceremony of any kind? I try to think of Franticek. I try to remember his kiss, but the fear is too big. It's swallowing me whole.

Now there is another plane coming toward me, headed right for where I am crouched on the ground. I flatten myself against the earth. Mother and Theo are with me, but all I can feel is my own heart beating.

Then, just like that, the airplanes take off, disappearing into the night sky as quickly as they came. My ears are still ringing. "It was just a way to frighten us," Frau Davidels whispers.

The night grows even darker. But wherever I look, I see the dim outlines of people.

"I heard one of the Nazis say there are already three hundred dead," a voice whispers. Some of the dead are elderly, too weak to last through the second census count. Some are trampled by the crowd. Some give up. The rest are shot.

When we file past the bodies, we turn our heads away. It is a sign of respect, but I know, too, that not to look at them is also a sign of cowardice. I don't have the courage to look at the corpses, to see their faces. It is too easy to imagine myself there with them on the wet grass.

At about four in the morning, an old man with a gray beard pushes his way through the crowd. "What do you want, old man?" someone asks. "Don't draw attention to yourself or they'll shoot you. Just like they did to that poor woman before."

When the old man turns toward us, I notice his eyes are bright blue. "I'm not afraid of being shot. Besides, I have something to tell you…a message you need to pass on to the others waiting in line."

"He's probably senile," a woman's voice calls out. "What does he know?"

"Hush," Fraulein Davidels tells the woman. "Don't you know who the old man is?"

"Why should I know him?" the woman answers.

"He's Rabbi Baeck—Leo Baeck—the chief rabbi of Berlin."

"What do rabbis know?" the woman continues.

"It's because of them and their religion we're in this mess."

"What is it you want to tell us, Rabbi Baeck?" Frau Davidels asks, raising her voice.

"Look up ahead," he says. We all look at the mass of bodies milling in front of us. "Do you see the stars?"

I look up at the sky, but the rabbi is wrong, there are no stars. Not one. Perhaps the stars witnessed what went on here tonight and decided not to shine.

Other people look up. When Rabbi Baeck speaks again, his voice sounds less patient. "Not up in the sky. Ahead of you!"

And suddenly I understand what Rabbi Baeck is talking about. Up ahead, extending all the way to the horizon are row after row of stars. Yellow ones—the stars we are forced to wear on our shirts and jackets.

"The stars meant to humiliate us Jews provide illumination in the gloom. They're a sign," Rabbi Baeck says.

"A sign of what?" the same woman who sounded so angry before asks.

"A sign we mustn't ever give up."

⚬

It is dawn when the Nazis finally let us leave the field. My eyelids ache from tiredness. When Theo stumbles, I stop to help him up. I'm too tired now to be angry with him.

Frau Davidels and Mother hold each other by the arm. Now that our ordeal is over, I start to think more clearly. That's when I realize I didn't see Hannelore during the census count. I hope she and her mother are all right.

When Frau Davidels yawns, I can see the gold crowns on her back teeth. Hannelore's mother told her that when prisoners die in Theresienstadt and are cremated, other prisoners are forced to scour the ashes in search of gold fillings. The thought makes me shiver.

A few strands of Frau Davidels' dark hair are stuck to her cheek. "It's nearly time to get to work," she tells me when she catches me looking at her.

"Work? Do you really think we'll have to work after the night we've had?"

Frau Davidels shakes her head. "It's inhuman to make us work after such a night, and that's precisely why they'll make us do it." She pats my shoulder. "Perhaps," she adds, "you'll have a chance to doze a little in your cauldron."

"Forty thousand." People are repeating the number, which is how many prisoners have been counted during the night. We knew the camp was overcrowded. But forty thousand prisoners crammed into a city built to house seven thousand! No wonder there is so little space and so little water! And though no one says it, we all know what the results of the census mean: Soon there will be another transport.

As Theo and I turn the corner onto Jagergasse, a woman with dark hair cranes her head to look at me. She holds a child in her arms, and another child, a little boy, is tugging on her long skirt. Why does the woman seem familiar? And then, all at once, I place her. It is Franticek's girlfriend, the one with whom I'd seen him go into the cubbyhole. I want to turn away, but I can't. I am too curious. How did she and her children manage during the census count? Where is her husband? And does she miss Franticek as much as I do?

Perhaps it is my imagination, but I think I catch her eyeing my necklace. Franticek's necklace.

I raise one hand to my neck and let my fingers take hold of the worn leather. There. If she did not notice the necklace before, she will notice it now.

Franticek touched this necklace. But then I realize with a start that he touched her too. I burn with jealousy. And then I remind myself what Franticek told me: that what he and this woman did together were "animal things." Those were his very words. There was nothing animal about *our* feelings for each other. It was different for Franticek and me.

To my surprise, the woman smiles at me. A small smile, but there is no question about it: she is smiling. I can't bring myself to smile back. In spite of what I've tried to tell myself, I am still jealous. She knows Franticek in a way I never did, in a way that perhaps I never shall.

When a few minutes later, Mother opens the door to our quarters and lets us in, I nearly weep. Not because I am sad. No, these are tears of joy. I am so relieved to be back in our miserable home. Eventually, every animal grows used to his cage.

Nine

"An old woman said…"

"Did you hear what the old woman said?"
Theresienstadt is full of old women. Even the women
who aren't old—Mother, Frau Davidels and Hannelore's
mother—all look old. But when people discuss what an
old woman has been saying, they aren't talking about
any one old woman. No. "An old woman said…" is camp
code. It means there is news.

So I prick up my ears one winter morning in 1944
when I hear two prisoners mention the old woman.
There is a layer of hard-packed snow on the ground,
and I am sipping coffee outside one of the kitchens near
our quarters. Only it isn't really coffee. It is what we call
ersatz, or make-believe, coffee. It is made of chicory and
has a mild grainy flavor. But like everyone else, I've long
forgotten the taste of real coffee. This at least warms my
fingers. I take small sips; bigger ones hurt my throat.

As I look around I think how coffee isn't all that
is make-believe at Theresienstadt. The whole camp is
make-believe. The stores are make-believe. The bank is

make-believe. And sometimes, it seems to me, even our hope is make-believe. People continue to say the end of the war is coming soon, but when they speak, I have the feeling they are only pretending to be hopeful. Making believe for the good of young people like me, and also for themselves.

So what does the old woman have to say?

Commandant Rahm has met with the Council of Elders. The Nazis have decided to introduce a new program: the Embellishment. I am puzzled. Embellishment? There is nothing "belle" (I know the word "embellishment" comes from the French word for beauty) about this vile gray place. Perhaps Father will know more. He's been back home with us for nearly a month. He still wobbles a little when he walks and when he comes home from the studio, I notice his fingers sometimes tremble. But the main thing is, he is able to do his work, and he's no longer on reduced rations.

So that night, when we are pulling the bedbugs off our blankets, I ask Father about the Embellishment. I can tell from the way Mother shakes out Theo's blanket that she and Father have already discussed the news.

Father sits down on the edge of my mattress. "The Nazis are expecting important visitors—representatives from the Danish Red Cross. They want Theresienstadt to appear to be the model city they've boasted about."

"That's crazy," I say. "Some model city! It's more like a model of misery, is what it is."

"There's good news," says Father. "Commandant Rahm has promised to make a number of improvements to the camp. We're supposed to get a playground for the children."

"With swing sets and a carousel?" Theo interrupts.

"I don't know about the carousel," Father says, "but it's likely there will be swing sets." When he smiles at Theo, Father's eyes look very sad.

"What else?" I ask Father.

"There's talk of flowerbeds and benches for prisoners to sit on."

I remember how I sipped my coffee standing up that morning. Benches will be nice. But then I consider how benches, flowerbeds and swing sets will do nothing to quell the hunger in our bellies. How ridiculous of the Nazis to spend money on frivolous things when everyone in Theresienstadt is starving!

"What about food?" I ask Father. "Will we be getting bigger rations? Real meat in our soup?"

"I haven't heard anything about food," Father admits.

"Food is what we need most," I tell him.

"But this is a start," he says.

It bothers me that Father is trying so hard to look at the bright side of things. Why can't he see that the Nazis are making a mockery of us?

Mother folds Theo's blanket over her arm. "I'm glad at least the Danish Red Cross cares about what's happening to us here," she says.

Father nods. "The Danish Red Cross is asking questions because of the trainload of Danish Jews who arrived here last month. But it looks as if their visit may improve conditions for the rest of us."

"It's not as if we can eat flowers," I mutter.

Then Theo, who rarely says anything that isn't annoying or just plain silly, surprises us all. "What about the Dutch Red Cross?" he wants to know. "Why haven't *they* come to visit?"

Father and Mother exchange a look. "The boy makes a good point," Father says.

I sigh. For the first time, I feel as if I've been abandoned by my own country. How could Holland let this happen to us? All this talk of embellishment only makes me feel worse. "Embellishment?" I cry out. "It's insane!"

Am I the only one who realizes how twisted our lives have become? To think we are excited about swing sets and benches and flowerbeds! Have we forgotten how hungry we are—and how others, like Franticek, have been shipped off to God only knows where? This Embellishment is just one more way for the Nazis to distract us from the truth: that we are wasting away in this miserable sick place.

Father breathes hard when he stands up. It's another aftereffect of the diphtheria. "It's true we can't eat flowers, Anneke," he says, "but we have to be practical. The Embellishment will mean more jobs for prisoners. And that buys us all something we desperately need."

"What's that?" I ask.

Father glances down at his left wrist. It's where he used to wear the watch that was taken away from him in the *Schleuse*. "Time," he says. "We're in desperate need of time."

∴𝑜𝑟

Within a week, there is a new sound in the camp: hammering. *Tap, tap, tap-a-tap-tap*. There is hammering everywhere. Near the main square, where Commandant Rahm has ordered the facades of more shops to be built, including a *bonbonnerie*. At the corner, where a café is being constructed—imagine, how preposterous: a café inside a prison!—and even outside our quarters, where a prisoner is installing a flowerbox made of rough-hewn planks.

The incessant hammering gives me a headache. Still, I have to admit that despite all my objections, the various improvements to the camp are not entirely unpleasant.

Even if it is all a sham, all part of a giant hoax, the improvements—and the work on the improvements—seems to be lifting people's spirits. "Do you think they'll send us geraniums for the flowerbox?" I hear Mother ask Father. "I so hope we'll have red geraniums. Tulips would be too much to ask for, what with the bulbs, but geraniums, especially bright red ones, would do me a world of good."

And yet, listening to Mother go on about red flowers also makes me want to scream. Doesn't she realize flowers won't do us any real good? What we need is food! Real food, not watery lentil soup and moldy bread! What we need is a way out of this place and an end to this awful war!

But there are moments when I, too, get caught up in plans for the Embellishment. I close my eyes and imagine myself and Hannelore at the café, listening to a concert. We've heard there will be weekly concerts for prisoners at the café.

"Do you think we'll have hot chocolate?" Theo asks, licking his cracked lips. And though I doubt it, I don't have the heart to tell him so.

Father is involved in the Embellishment too. He has been commissioned by Commandant Rahm himself to decorate the walls of the children's infirmary. The commandant has requested, of all things, a fairy-tale motif. When one night, Father tells us about it, I laugh out loud. "Bah!" I say. "Fairy tales! A painting of a graveyard would be a better choice!"

Father gives me a stern look. "Anneke," he says, "remember what I told you."

Father has already completed one mural of Rapunzel with her long blond hair streaming out of the tower where she was imprisoned by a terrible witch.

"Anneke's right," I hear Father tell Mother later when the curtain that separates us is drawn. "It is bizarre to be painting fairy-tale scenes in a place like this." I'm glad that at least in private, Father shares my opinion.

Mother makes a tut-tutting sound. "Perhaps your murals will bring the sick children a little joy." How can Mother really believe the Embellishment has some value?

Doesn't she see the Nazis are trying to trick not only the Danish Red Cross, but us as well?

Father sighs. "You may be right. Besides, Rapunzel is a hopeful story. She found a way out of her prison. I sometimes wonder, Tineke"—Father lowers his voice to a whisper—"whether we'll *ever* find a way out." My shoulders tense up. It isn't like Father to sound so discouraged. How can he, of all people, be losing hope? The thought makes me feel unmoored.

But then I hear Mother's voice, soft and strong. "Jo," she says, "you'll always be my handsome prince."

"I was just a frog until you kissed me."

Mother laughs. "Now, Jo, you're mixing up your fairy-tales."

I hear them shift a little on their mattress.

I have so many worries on my mind: Franticek, this crazy Embellishment and my sense that I am the only one who understands we are being duped. Yet the sound of Mother's laughter stays with me as I drift off to sleep.

"Your father is working too hard on those murals," Mother tells me one afternoon soon after that. She twists some strands of dark hair around her index finger. "I worry about him."

I reach into my apron pocket and take out the potato Frau Davidels has just given me. It is small and misshapen, but I know Mother will be pleased. "I'm going to boil it up straightaway," she says, glad, as usual, to have some task to keep her occupied. "Then you can deliver it to the children's infirmary."

Father is standing on a chair, using a thick pencil to draw a giant frog on the wall across from the doctors' station. He is concentrating so hard on getting the warts on the frog's back right, he doesn't notice me coming down the hallway.

"Father!" I call out, looking around to see no one is in earshot. "Mother asked me to deliver this." She has packed three thin slices of boiled potato inside her enamel cup. Theo and I have already eaten our share. Mother didn't want any. "I'm not hungry," she said when she sliced the potato. Of course, I know it isn't true.

Father's face brightens. My stomach rumbles as I watch him pop the first slice into his mouth. I am so hungry it hurts. "You take this one," he says, offering me the second slice.

I remember how Mother said she was worried about

Father. "I've already had my share," I tell him, looking away.

On my way out, I see two doctors. I know they are Jewish because I've seen them in the soup line with the rest of us. They are outside one of the small rooms they use to perform operations. "Now that we've set the bone, the child will likely walk without a limp," one of the doctors says to the other.

I smile as I pass them. I want them to know I am grateful for everything they do. It's a blessing the child they're discussing won't have a limp.

They are standing in front of the Rapunzel mural. Rapunzel's hair looks so thick and blond I can practically feel its coarse texture. I have an urge to tell them my father painted her, but I am too shy. Just then, the younger of the two turns toward the mural, looking at it as if he is noticing it for the first time. "Part of the Embellishment," he says, rolling his eyes. "Designed so that when the Danish Red Cross visits, its representatives will be impressed by the looks of our fine infirmary."

My urge to tell them that the mural is my father's work disappears. So I am not the only one who disapproves of the Embellishment. Why else would this doctor roll his eyes?

"We're living in an insane world," his colleague observes.

I suck in my breath. I'm right, then, to be suspicious of the Embellishment. These men are doctors, scientists; they must know the truth.

"What's most insane isn't this new wall decoration,"
the first doctor says. "What's most insane is that the
Nazis ask us to treat children, only to dispose of them in
the death camps."

Death camps? My whole body begins to shudder.
What has the doctor just said? For a moment, I wonder
if perhaps I have misheard him. But no! He said children
are disposed of in death camps. "Disposed of." Those
are words people use to talk about garbage, not human
beings. Not children. Can it be true? It must be true!
What would this man stand to gain by lying?

My breath seems to be trapped in my throat. I must
have made a choking sound because one of the doctors
asks whether I am all right. "Young woman," he says,
"you look like you are about to faint."

I push him away. I am too upset to speak. So the
rumors about the death camps are true. My Franticek,
I think. My Franticek!

As I rush out of the infirmary, I am filled with the
terrible unwavering certainty that Franticek is dead.
Gone, vanished. And somehow, my life has gone on
without him.

When I get outside, my legs give way, and I collapse
on the ground, weeping. The sobbing makes my body
shake and my throat hurt. No one stops to ask me what
is wrong. In Theresienstadt, a weeping girl is not an
unusual sight.

While Hannelore and I wait in line for our miserable ladle of lentil soup (it isn't even made from real lentils, just some awful dried lentil powder), we survey the changes taking place around us.

There are poplar saplings in the central square. Several apartments have flowerboxes like ours. Mother never did get her red geraniums. She has settled for some scruffy-looking greenery. Mother says it is better than nothing. "Green," she tells me, "is the color of life."

I don't have the heart to tell her that maybe nothing would have been better. At least that way she wouldn't be fooled into thinking that conditions in the camp are really improving.

The poplar saplings and Mother's plants aren't the only new additions to the camp that are green. There are also squares of green grass that prisoners have been made to plant in the dirt. At first, the bright green color gives us a shock. We've grown so used to the gray and brown shades that are everywhere in Theresienstadt. Gray and brown bricks, and of course, gray faces. But within a few days, despite the prisoners' best efforts to water the turf, it begins to turn first yellow, then brown.

The same thing, I think, is happening to us. If, as Mother says, green is the color of life, we are turning gray and brown here too. Nothing can stay green in Theresienstadt.

And though the camp is being embellished—there are a few new benches, a playground with three seesaws, a monument in the main square, and the bunk beds in the barracks have been cut down so there are two tiers of beds, not three—only the surface of our world has changed. We are still starving. We are still in danger of being sent on one of the transports. Death still stares us in the eye.

"Can you imagine a *bonbonnerie* without bonbons?" Hannelore asks. "It's criminal."

"Did you ever taste Dutch licorice?" I ask her. My mouth waters at the memory of the salty sweet taste. It is a kind of game we prisoners sometimes play—remembering our favorite foods from our old lives.

Hannelore wrinkles her nose. "I hate licorice! I always preferred tortes—especially my Tante Helga's *nusstorte*. She uses hazelnuts instead of flour. And mocha cream. Oh, it's so good I can almost taste it!"

"You don't like licorice?" I poke Hannelore's stomach. When I do, I notice how her ribs protrude from her side. "Something tells me if someone came around this instant and offered you a piece of Dutch licorice, you'd be glad of it."

Hannelore turns away. "You're probably right," she concedes.

Talking about foods we've eaten in the past brings a momentary pleasure, but such conversations have a price. Afterward, we feel even hungrier than before. My belly is so empty it hurts. Sometimes my stomach makes odd gurgling noises as if it is complaining of neglect.

No, all in all, it is better not to remember food and not to talk about it. So I try to change the subject. "This Embellishment," I say to Hannelore, "makes me think of Potemkin Village."

Hannelore nods. "Yes, indeed. You're quite right. We learned about Potemkin in school. He was the Russian minister who had his troops construct a pretend village along the banks of the Dnieper River."

"I can't for the life of me remember Potemkin's first name. Can you?" I ask her.

Hannelore scrunches her forehead. She can't remember it either.

"It's the hunger," Hannelore says, shaking her head, "it's beginning to affect our brains."

"Or maybe we weren't paying attention in class! Maybe you were too busy mooning over Gunter!"

It's good to see Hannelore laugh.

That night the soup is so thin and there is so little of it that I weep. I know I shouldn't cry. There are far worse things than being hungry. But I can't help it. The long days in the diet kitchen, the hunger and the sadness are wearing me down. So when Hannelore and I finish slurping our soup, and we are sitting together on one of the new benches, I take my spoon and use it to scrape at the inside of my cup. The enamel begins to fall off in tiny silver slivers. And because I am so hungry, I eat it.

Hannelore, who is just as hungry, follows my example. The enamel tastes sharp and metallic, but at least those little slivers mean there is something in our empty stomachs.

We don't say much on the way back. I think we both feel ashamed that we've eaten the enamel bits. What if we get sick? Then all at once, Hannelore grabs my arm. My first thought is that she is suffering the first effects of poisoning. It will be all my fault. But it isn't that at all.

"Grigori!" she says excitedly. "His name was Grigori Potemkin!"

Ten

*H*annelore and her mother are gone.

But I can't cry. It takes energy to mourn the loss of someone you love. Energy to cry. Energy to remember all the things that were, all the things you took for granted. The times you laughed together, the stories and secrets you shared, even the times you cried together. All of the last moments. The last time the two of you walked down the road on the side of the central square—the narrow road reserved for Jews. The last time you waited together in line for ersatz coffee or lentil soup. The last time you stood together as darkness fell, looking up at the stars and making a wish.

It takes energy to think of all the moments that will never be. The letters we would never exchange when this insanity is over. If it will ever truly be over...

But I don't have the energy for any of this. My throat hurts too much, my belly is too empty. And my heart feels empty. If I lay my hand on my breast, I can feel my heart beating away, but I know the truth. It is just an organ. Inside, my heart has become as hollow as my belly.

The tears won't come even when I try to force them by squinting my eyes. Besides, I know I haven't the right to cry. I haven't suffered more than anyone else in Theresienstadt. In fact, I've suffered less. We are, after all, the lucky ones.

But being lucky is a burden all its own. Those of us who remain in Theresienstadt must bear witness when others leave.

If the tears do come, I know they'll only upset Father and Mother and Theo.

We have to be strong for each other. We tell each other sometimes that it takes strength not to cry. But part of me isn't so sure. Could the opposite also be true? Might it take strength to cry, to consider all that was and will never be?

But I am too weak for that.

The Embellishment is not just a matter of flower-boxes and turf and seesaws. No, it has required several more transports, each of one thousand more souls. After all, what will the Danish delegation think if they see a city so crowded with people there is no place to turn, no room to breathe?

I've stopped believing that any of them—Franticek, Hannelore, her uncle, her mother and all the thousands of others—are in a better place. I can't forget what I heard the Jewish doctor say about the death camps.

The old woman is talking again. "Did you hear what the old woman said?" voices ask as I make my way early one morning to the diet kitchen.

A group of children arrived in the middle of last night. They are from Bialystok, Poland, and their arrival at the camp is to be kept top secret. Though, of course, that isn't too likely to happen in Theresienstadt. Not in a place with such a talkative old woman.

The orphans are whisked off to a separate barracks at the edge of the camp. No one is to see them or speak to them.

But I see them. Frau Davidels chooses me to deliver their soup and slices of stale brown bread. "Keep your eyes down," she tells me, "and don't say a word. There will be Nazi soldiers everywhere and you mustn't draw attention to yourself, Anneke. Deliver the soup and the bread, then come directly back." She eyes the clock on the wall in the diet kitchen. "I'll expect you in twenty minutes then."

The soup is in a metal tureen, so I need both hands to carry it; Frau Davidels strings a burlap sack full of bread over my shoulder. I walk toward the barracks where the orphans are. Poor things. They have nobody left. No father, no mother. My throat, already sore, aches even more when I think of them.

Four Nazis are stationed outside the barracks. Their rifles hang slackly across their chests.

"Leave the food right here, you Jew bitch!" one of them says, pointing with his gun to a spot on the ground.

When I stumble a little, one of the Nazis laughs.

I hope I haven't spilled any soup. The orphans must be very hungry.

I hear movement inside the barracks. Little bodies shuffling. I imagine the orphans trying to make sense of their new surroundings.

"Get going!" shouts the Nazi who called me Jew bitch.

But before I reach the first corner on my way back to the diet kitchen, I hear noise—lots of it—coming from the barracks where the orphans are. Though I know I'm not supposed to, I slow down and turn my head just a little to see what is going on. The orphans are filing out of the barracks. There is a sea of dark heads and ragged clothing.

A German voice pierces the air. "To the showers!" the voice says. "All of you! *Raus!*"

Then I hear a terrible whimpering. It starts out low and small, but it quickly grows loud and desperate. "No! No!" I hear little voices call out. The voices are trembling, but the words are clear. "Don't send us to the gas, please, no!" they plead.

Gas? I think, struggling to make sense of the children's cries. Showers? Gas? What do they mean? And then, suddenly, I begin to understand. I cover my mouth with my hand. There is nothing in my stomach, but I feel as if I am about to retch.

I imagine Hannelore and Franticek standing outside some building marked *Showers*. But there are no showers inside. There is some terrible contraption instead, something wicked, designed to kill Jews, to gas us to death. The orphans must have seen this. No wonder they are so afraid! And no wonder their presence must be kept top secret.

These children have not just lost their parents. These children have been at a death camp, perhaps the dreaded Auschwitz.

··∞

I work, I eat, I line up for ersatz coffee and lentil soup, I battle the bedbugs. But part of me has disappeared, leapt out of my body for good after Hannelore left on the transport and I heard the orphans' fearful cries.

One Sunday afternoon, a group of young Czech prisoners tries to persuade me to come with them to the top of one of the barracks on Jagergasse. "You have to see the view from there," one of the boys tells me. His accent upsets me. It reminds me of Franticek. "You can see for kilometers and kilometers."

"I'm too tired." Besides, I don't want to see for kilometers and kilometers. If I do, I'll only be reminded that I am trapped here in Theresienstadt. That will make me feel even worse than I already do.

Mother, who is darning one of Theo's socks when the young people come knocking, urges me to go. "A change of scenery may do you good."

"Let's go!" says a girl named Gizela, who has frizzy brown hair that looks like a wooly cap. She reaches for my hand. I can tell she is the sort of person who is used to getting her way.

And so, reluctantly, I follow Gizela and her friends.

The barracks, which are just down the street from our apartment, stink. But the young Czechs pay no attention. They hurry up the narrow wooden stairway at the far end of the barracks.

I stop to take a breath when I reach the attic. "Come on!" says the boy who sounds like Franticek. "There's still another staircase."

I gasp when a cold bony hand touches the small of my back. When I spin around, I see a face so pale it seems to shine in the dark. It belongs to an old woman. The bones on her face protrude under her papery skin. She looks more dead than alive. I draw back from her as if I am afraid to catch whatever she has got.

"Do you have anything for me to eat? Anything?" she asks. I can barely feel her fingers on my back, they are so thin.

I know that many of the old people in Theresienstadt have been forced to live in the attics. Chances are, of course, the Danish delegation will never come all the way up here to inspect the condition of the camp. But I have never seen someone look so old and ill.

"I'm sorry," I stammer. "I haven't anything for you." In the dim light, I can see other old people lying, crumpled like paper bags, on the floor. One makes a low moaning sound. I want to run away.

There is nothing I can do for them. I have no food to share. I am filled with a terrible sense of helplessness. The way this old woman is looking at me, reaching for me, her eyes filled with desperation, only makes me feel more helpless. So when I hear Gizela call my name, I turn and hurry up the stairs. The old woman whimpers. I blink hard. I have to make the picture of those old people go away.

Gizela and the others are already on the edge of the roof, pointing at the countryside. "Look! The trees are coming back to life! See their yellow-green color!" Gizela says. Her arms are as thin as mine. It seems to bother her that I am not more excited. "Come, Anneke! Come look!"

"Okay, okay," I tell her. It is the first time in nearly a year that I've seen anything beyond Theresienstadt and the tall dreary ramparts surrounding it.

I look and see the yellow-green that Gizela is talking about, and I see the round hills and shallow valleys in the distance. They seem to stretch out forever.

Another girl is lying on her back, gazing upward. "Look at the sky. There's not a cloud."

I see the sky too. She's right. There's not a cloud.

But none of what I see touches me. The sun is out, but I don't feel its warmth. The others say they can hear a bird chirping, but I don't. Gizela shrugs when she looks at me; then she turns back to her friends.

In my heart, it is another gray day. I feel as if the gray in my heart will never go away.

✺

"I'm worried about Anneke," I hear Mother whisper from behind the curtain. It is very late, and she and Father must think I am asleep. But it is as if I've become incapable of sleep. Sometimes, I toss on my mattress, slapping at the bedbugs. Lately, I've been trying a new strategy: I lie perfectly still and let them bite me. Sometimes, I pretend to be dead. If I am dead, the bugs can't do me any harm, and the sadness will stop. If I am dead, perhaps I can be with Franticek and Hannelore.

"What can we do for her?" Father asks.

"I don't know," Mother says. Then I hear a deep sigh, followed by the sound of one of them shifting on their mattress.

"Shh," I hear Mother say. "We mustn't wake the children."

✺

Father is putting the finishing touches on his mural of *The Ugly Duckling*. "The story of *The Ugly Duckling* is a little like Commandant Rahm's Embellishment, only the changes here are purely on the surface," Petr Kien says one afternoon when he and his wife pass by our quarters. I'm glad there's someone else who agrees with me.

"But there have been some real changes," his wife insists.

Petr Kien raises his eyebrows. "Do you mean the flowerboxes?"

"No, I mean the extra hour of rest time they've given us on Sunday afternoons. And the fact they haven't objected when that rabbi from Germany, the one with the long beard, addresses members of his old congregation. As long as there aren't too many people."

"Bah!" Father says. "The old man is selling snake oil."

An image of Rabbi Baeck's face flashes through my mind—his piercing blue eyes and his beard that is so long and bushy it looks as if birds could nest in it. I remember him from the night of the census count, the night I thought things couldn't get any worse. Of course I realize now that I was wrong.

⁘

The following Sunday, I announce I am going for a walk.

Father and Mother forget to ask where I am headed. I know it is because they are so glad to see me leave the apartment. Since Hannelore's departure, I've spent almost every Sunday afternoon inside, lying on my mattress, staring up at the ceiling.

I know where to look for the rabbi: On Sunday afternoons, the German Jews tend to gather in one of the smaller squares. Sure enough, when I arrive, Rabbi Baeck is holding court. Someone has brought him a rickety chair to sit on, and a group of German prisoners is gathered round him, listening to him speak. Though his voice is frail, there is something musical about it.

"'The Lord giveth and the Lord taketh away, bless'd be the name of the Lord.' These words," Rabbi Baeck says, "appear in the *Book of Job*. It teaches us that, like Job, we cannot expect to understand the ways of the Lord."

People nod wisely, and when he looks up, Rabbi Baeck's eyes settle on me. I would like to say something. Ask how God, if He exists, could simply stand by when Franticek and Hannelore were sent off on transports. But I don't dare. If they hear my Dutch accent, everyone will know I am an outsider.

Besides, perhaps Father is right, and Rabbi Baeck is selling snake oil. But I suppose that if his words help the people who come to hear him speak, then there is no harm in it.

As I walk back to our apartment, I decide not to tell Father and Mother where I've been. And I think about that line from the *Book of Job*. The Lord has taken so much away from me. I don't think I can ever bless his name.

Eleven

*O*pa, my grandfather, is being transferred to Theresienstadt.

Father learned from Dutch Jews, who arrived after us, that shortly after we were deported from Holland, my opa was sent east on a transport. Father rarely mentions his father, but when he does, he casts his eyes to the ground. I know that means he misses him. Father's mother died when he was a child, and so he grew very close to his father.

"I didn't dare hope he was still alive," Father tells us the evening the news comes.

It is Commandant Rahm's doing. Though it's hard to believe, perhaps the man is not entirely evil. Father explains how, two weeks before, Rahm asked if Father had, by any chance, an elderly relative by the name of Zacharias Van Raalte. Commandant Rahm had seen this Zacharias's name on a list of prisoners in a camp called Bergen-Belsen. When Father explained that Zacharias Van Raalte was our opa, Rahm said he would try to have him transferred to Theresienstadt so he could be with us. "At least this way," Rahm told Father, "I'll have done one decent thing during this war."

"Did he really say that?" I ask. Somehow, it is easier for me to think of Rahm as a monster.

"Why didn't you tell us Opa might be coming?" Mother asks. From the way she raises her voice I know she means to reproach Father for keeping a secret from her.

"I didn't want to build up your hopes, or mine," Father says in a quiet voice. "But Commandant Rahm seems fairly certain Father will be arriving here today. And I can't keep the secret any longer."

We can't wait to see Opa! He was always such fun. Unlike most grandfathers, ours lived in a hotel, and a glamorous one at that. There were velvet chairs in the lobby and a doorman in a fur hat. Mother said Opa lived in a hotel because he had no wife and needed looking after. When we used to visit him in Zutphen, we got to stay in the hotel. Once, Theo and I had a room of our own. We pretended we were travelers come all the way from Broek for an adventure.

Opa was also a dapper dresser. Even on weekends, he wore a wool suit and tie. And he was a great billiards player. There was a billiards table in his hotel, and he tried to teach Theo and me to play. "You've got a good eye," I remember him telling me. "As for you, Theo, you'll have to grow a few more centimeters in order to see the top of the table."

It was no secret, either, that Opa liked ladies. We often arrived at the hotel to find him sitting at a table in the lobby, surrounded by a group of women. They'd admire his fine clothes and giggle at his stories. One of them, her name was Lotje, was almost always there when we visited.

Lotje was pretty for an old lady, with bluish gray hair and pink cheeks. "They're only friends," I once heard Father tell Mother, but I knew it wasn't true. Once I'd walked into Opa's room and found him kissing Lotje on the lips. I'd never told Father and Mother. Opa, I decided, was entitled to some fun. Besides, I liked Lotje. She almost always slipped a bar of Droste orange-flavored chocolate into my satchel. "Our little secret," she'd whisper, putting her pointer finger over her mouth.

I wonder what became of Lotje. I never thought to ask whether she was Jewish. I hope, for her sake, that she isn't, and that she is still at the hotel, waiting for Opa to come back to her.

That evening, the four of us get special permission to meet the train. Jewish prisoners have extended the railway tracks, so there is now a small station inside Theresienstadt. At least Opa won't have to make the two-kilometer walk from Buhosovice the way we had to.

Mother combs my hair and Theo's. "Stand up straight. Shoulders back," she tells me as we spot a train in the distance. Father strains to get a better look.

The chugging noises come closer, and when the train finally pulls up to the platform, we rush over to the first door. A group of old people tumbles out.

The first thing I notice is their smell. It's so foul I want to pinch my nose. These old people are dressed in filthy rags. I'm reminded of the old people I saw in the attic on Jagergasse. Only these ones look even worse.

Father shifts from one foot to the other. "I don't see him," he says.

I stand on my tiptoes to help look for Opa. I look for a tall man with strong shoulders, but all of the men who step off the train are hunched over and ancient-looking. One's face is covered in stubble. That can't be my opa, whose face is always shaved clean and smells lemony.

Father sighs. "Perhaps Rahm was only toying with me," he tells Mother. I think how that would be just like the Nazis, who seem to come up with every possible way to make us miserable. I can feel my hatred for them coursing through my veins like blood.

But Mother won't give up. She pushes her way into the small crowd, getting so close to the new arrivals her face nearly touches theirs. "I've found him!" she calls out at last. "I've found him!"

Father rushes over to where Mother is standing, and Theo and I follow as quickly as we can. I'm so excited I could burst. In a moment, I will be reunited with my opa!

But how can this little crumpled man be Opa?

Has he shrunk?

Father begins to weep. He has taken Opa into his arms and is rocking him gently.

The first thing I notice are the dirty paper plasters on Opa's hands and face. Did he contract some sort of skin disease at Bergen-Belsen? Though it isn't kind of me, I can't help hoping that whatever is wrong with him is not contagious. After all, Father and Mother told me I'd be sharing my side of the room with Opa.

There is no point sending these new arrivals to the *Schleuse* since they are not carrying anything of value. Opa doesn't even have a rucksack of his own. Later, when we help him undress, we find an enamel cup in his coat pocket. Like mine, it has been scraped clean.

·ⁱᵉ⌒

As soon as we get Opa to the apartment, Mother begins barking orders. "Anneke, see if Frau Davidels can help us find some fresh water. Even a cup or two will do. Theo, pull the bedbugs off Anneke's blanket. Jo, don't just stand there gawking, get your father a sugar cube. Something sweet might do him good."

Father puts the sugar cube on Opa's tongue and pats his forehead as if he is Opa's father, and not the other way around.

Opa is too tired and sick to speak. I nearly vomit when Mother peels off the plasters—underneath, his skin is covered in boils. Yellowish pus leaks out from some of them. Father turns pale at the sight, but Mother keeps working, dabbing at the boils with a cloth she's dipped in the water Frau Davidels supplied.

Theo and I help Father cut new plasters from a piece of old newsprint.

"Opa stinks," Theo whispers, curling up his nose.

Father is too busy handing Mother plasters to reprimand Theo.

Soon, Opa is sound asleep, snoring lightly on my mattress. Though he is far more wrinkled than he was before the war, there is something almost childlike about his expression.

I can tell from the way Father is wringing his hands that he is worried. Mother notices too. "He'll be fine, Jo," she tells him. "Just wait and see."

When Theo and I get up the next morning, Opa is still asleep. "Do you think he's dead?" Theo asks.

"Of course not. He's breathing. Look at the way his chest is moving up and down."

Father and Mother peek out from behind the curtain. The four of us gather around Opa. He must feel our presence because just then, he wakes up. I see his eyes meet Father's and Mother's, then mine and Theo's. He blinks a few times, as if he isn't sure he can trust his own vision. Then he rubs at his eyes.

When he speaks, his voice is weak. "Tell me," he asks us, his eyes wet with tears, "am I—could I be—by any chance—in Heaven?"

Twelve

One thing I'm learning is that even during terrible times, life finds a way of settling into a routine. I grow accustomed to sharing my mattress and blanket with Opa. At first, when he snores, I whisper and ask him to stop. When that doesn't work—and when Opa gets a little stronger—I use the back of my hand to smack his arm. Which usually puts a quick end to his snoring!

Opa rarely speaks about Bergen-Belsen, and when he tries to, Father and Mother give him a stern look. I know it is because they want to protect us.

Because Opa is considered too old to work, he spends his days resting in the apartment. Thank goodness he is living with us, and not in an attic like the one I saw.

The numbness I've been feeling doesn't go away. Instead I become accustomed to it. I sometimes wonder where the old Anneke has gone and if I'll ever meet her again. Somehow I doubt it.

Opa makes Theo a soccer ball from rags he ties together. "I'd have preferred to make a billiards table, but this was all I could manage," Opa jokes when he gives Theo the ball.

Theo is delighted. Whenever they can, he and the other boys who live nearby kick the ball around the narrow courtyard behind our apartment. From inside, I can hear the steady thud of the ball as it hits the wall. One child always stands guard at the corner; the boys know if the Nazis catch them playing, the precious ball will almost certainly be confiscated.

It is May, and according to the old woman, the Danish Red Cross will be arriving before the end of summer. Some spindly white and yellow flowers sprout in our flowerbox. One evening, Father and Mother attend a concert at the café.

It may be the Embellishment, or perhaps it's the soft spring air, but we prisoners almost start to believe things really are getting a little better for us. Sometimes I feel as if we are performing in a huge play, and we're beginning to take on our stage roles.

But all that changes the morning the black limousine pulls up again in front of Commandant Rahm's headquarters. A few hours later, the Council of Elders is summoned. It seems as if the whole camp shudders when we learn the news: There will be another transport, the biggest in the history of Theresienstadt. In order that the camp not appear overcrowded when the Danish delegation makes its visit, seven thousand prisoners will be sent east in three days time. Seven thousand! And for some reason none of us understand, Theo's name is on the list.

Opa is the one who tells me. He is alone in the apartment when the notice arrives. When I come back from the diet kitchen, he is waving a narrow slip of paper at me. His hands are shaking.

I start to shake. My first thought is that Opa's name is on the notice. How can anyone be so cruel, to send him back to us only to take him away again? I stretch open my arms. Opa collapses against me, sobbing.

"I know your parents will say I shouldn't tell you, but I don't know what else to do. The poor boy is only eleven years old."

At first, Opa's words make no sense. What poor boy is he talking about? Theo is eleven. Can Opa be talking about Theo? I feel the muscles around my heart clench. This can't be!

Theo is outside playing soccer. The ball bounces against the wall. "We mustn't say a word to him," I tell Opa.

He wipes his eyes. "Of course not."

As soon as they walk into the apartment, Father and Mother seem to know something is wrong. Mother bursts into tears at the news. Father's face grows very pale, but he doesn't say a word.

Opa stands up. "I'm going to go in Theo's place," he says as he reaches for his coat.

Father pushes Opa back onto the bench where he was sitting. "You'll do nothing of the sort. You'll only make things worse." I know Father is remembering what happened to Herr Adler when he tried to save his artists.

When Opa bows his head, I wonder if there will ever come a day when I will order Father and Mother about. But perhaps I'll never live to be that old. If Theo's name is on this transport list, who's to say my name won't be on the next one? Though the May air is warm, I suddenly feel a terrible chill. I know it's fear. Pure fear.

Theo comes rushing up the stairway to our quarters. "Did you score a goal?" I ask him. It is hard to keep my voice from breaking.

Theo's cheeks are flushed from running. "No, I scored three!" He sticks out his tongue and shakes his head. It is the sort of silly gesture that would usually irritate me.

But when he does it now, I think my heart might crack open inside my chest. I've never really gotten on with Theo. All my life, I've seen him mostly as a pest, and there have certainly been times when I wished him gone. If only I could take all those times back! In fact, I have a terrible suspicion—one that is too shameful to share with anyone now that Hannelore is gone: I feel as if somehow it is my fault that Theo's name is on the transport list. I wished him gone so many times that now my wish is coming true. My body aches with guilt. This guilt is even more awful than the fear. I can feel it weighing me down, pressing against my shoulders and my spine.

Despite his sometimes annoying behavior, I know Theo is a good boy. He is my brother, my only sibling, and I don't know if I will be able to carry on without him. But I also know I mustn't cry in front of him.

Theo seems not to notice the tension in the apartment. Mother's eyes are rimmed in red, Opa is nibbling on his thumbnail and Father is pacing in front of the window.

"Do you think I can go out again later to meet the boys and play more soccer?" Theo asks.

"I don't see why not," Mother tells him. I can tell she is holding back her tears.

"I have to see Dr. Epstein," Father announces. "About the murals," he adds as an afterthought.

Of course, I know the bit about the murals isn't true. Father is going to join the queue of people waiting outside the Council of Elders headquarters. He is going to beg for Theo's life.

~~~

I've always been the sort of person who wants to know everything, but I think sometimes it's better not to know. We can't let Theo know that his name is on the list.

After Father leaves, Theo babbles on about soccer. One of the other boys wants to become a professional soccer player, and Theo wonders whether we think that is possible. And if it is, whether Theo might become one too.

Opa swallows hard before speaking. His Adam's apple moves back and forth inside his skinny neck like a ping-pong ball. "It's a fine idea," Opa says, keeping his eyes firmly planted on Theo, as if he can't bear to let him out of his sight.

"What do you think, Anneke?" Theo asks.

For once, I haven't the heart to insult him. "I think you'll make a splendid soccer player."

"You do?" Theo grins. But then he gives me an odd look. I know he isn't used to my being nice to him. That makes me feel even worse.

Theo is humming to himself when we leave for the soup line. There is still no sign of Father. Mother draws Theo close as we join the line. There is a dullness to her eyes I haven't seen before.

Everyone is talking about the upcoming transport, speculating about who will be sent away. "Old decrepit people," someone says. "The Nazis won't want the Red Cross to be disgusted."

"Young people," someone counters. "Because they'd make the Red Cross feel too sorry for them."

Mother stiffens. Theo makes no more mention of his soccer-playing plans.

I wonder if he knows.

That night, after Theo goes to sleep in the bathtub, I pray again. This time, I think I'll try pressing my palms together. Maybe God will hear me better. I don't care what Mother or Opa will say, and Father can't say anything because he is still waiting for his audience with Dr. Epstein.

Opa is lying on his side of the mattress, staring up at the ceiling and making sniffling sounds. Because his hearing is poor, I think he may not notice if I whisper my request to God. I raise my hands to my chest and drop down my head. "Please, dear God, please save Theo." And because I think it might also help my cause if I offer God something in exchange, I add, "If you save Theo, I promise never to say another cross word to him. And never to ask you for anything else again."

But Opa does hear me, or notices what I am up to, because a moment later, he lifts himself up from the mattress and comes to kneel beside me. And then, to my surprise, Mother pokes her head out from behind the curtain and joins us too.

The three of us kneel on the floor together, hands joined. We bow our heads, though none of us says a word.

If there is a God—and I have never hoped more desperately that there is—and He is capable of understanding what goes on inside people's hearts, why then, he has to hear our prayer.

That thought makes it a little easier to fall asleep.

When I get up in the morning, Father is back. He is putting on his khaki-colored work shirt. His face looks strained, but when he nods his head at me, I know the news is good.

Father doesn't tell us what he said to Dr. Epstein to persuade him to remove Theo's name from the list. But sometimes I think Theo suspects the truth. Perhaps he figured out why I was being kind to him, why Opa sniffled in his sleep, why Mother looked so unhappy and Father was in such a hurry to see Dr. Epstein. I try to imagine how afraid Theo must have felt. But no matter how hard I try, I can't imagine it. It's too big even for my imagination.

Later that morning, Theo is quieter than usual, but by the end of the afternoon, he is back to his old tricks. He pokes me in the belly. "They're trying to starve us, but you're still a fatso, Anneke," he says. My blood boils, but because I am determined to keep my promise, I don't give him the smack I'd like to.

On the morning of the transport, I sneak out of my cauldron. Not that Frau Davidels will notice. With so many people leaving on this transport, those of us who remain all know someone who is being shipped out, and we are eager to say a last few words or give one final kiss.

Though people are bustling about, the mood in Theresienstadt is somber. People say little. I feel like an actress in a silent movie.

Like everyone else, I walk in the direction of the train platform. Only a few weeks ago, we came here to collect Opa. But now, with so many people milling around—those who are leaving on the transport and those who have come to see them off—I can't get within two blocks of the platform. So I stand on the corner and watch the silent movie unfold.

Many of those who are departing adjust their rucksacks. Though they are leaving Theresienstadt with far less than they came with, they fuss over their meager belongings: a change of clothes, a frayed photograph— the frame, if it had had any value, confiscated long ago at the *Schleuse*—a tin cup, a fork. There is no need for knives since we never have food substantial enough to require cutting. Some cast a final look back at the camp that has been their temporary home. Others simply head for the train.

Those of us who have come to see them off do our best to be brave. "I know we'll be together soon," I hear a woman tell an older man. But when he is out of sight, the woman bursts into tears, her shoulders heaving as she sobs.

After the train pulls out of the camp and I am returning to the diet kitchen, I notice a girl my age wiping her cheeks with the backs of her hands. I'd like to comfort her, but I don't have the strength.

There's no room in my heart for a new friend. Besides, all friendships here end badly. Sooner or later, one of us will end up on a transport.

Something else stops me from talking to this girl. It is a terrible thought: What if she is crying because her little brother is on the transport, sent to take Theo's place?

.:ö~

"What is it?" I ask Father when he hands me the little square of brown paper.

Mother stands next to him, her arm on his forearm. Theo and Opa are on Father's other side.

"Have you forgotten what day it is?" Opa asks, his blue eyes twinkling.

"What day it is?" I look out the window as if the view might provide an answer. The light has grown a little stronger.

I know it's May. What day exactly, I'm not sure. Then all at once, I understand why Father and Mother and Theo and Opa are gathered around me. To think I'd nearly forgotten my own birthday!

"You got me a present?" I say, rubbing the little square between my fingers and trying to guess what is inside. It is something flat and hard. I resist the urge to tear off the paper. It has been so long since I received a present. I want to savor every moment.

"It's from all of us," Theo says, "but Father made it."

It is just like Theo to try and ruin my surprise. I flash him a stern look. It is getting harder every day to keep the promise I made God.

Tucked inside the brown paper is a tiny square metal frame, not much larger than my thumbnail. I see the back of the frame first. It is engraved with the numbers 24-V-1944: my fifteenth birthday. Where did Father find an engraver?

I flip the frame over and when I do, my heart nearly stops. There, in miniature, is a portrait of Broek. I'd know it anywhere. The church with its tall steeple in the background, a giant poplar tree to the left, and in front just behind the little wooden picket fence, our clapboard house.

I don't ask Father why he chose to draw a winter scene. The poplar tree is bare, the roof of our house and the church are covered in a thick layer of snow, like white icing on a cake.

Father's drawing is behind a little piece of glass someone has measured and cut exactly so it can slide inside the frame. And on top of the frame, perfectly centered, is a simple metal hook.

I unfasten Franticek's strip of leather from around my neck. Carefully I untie the double knot that keeps my necklace closed and slip the leather through the hook.

Father looks on approvingly. "I thought you might want to wear it on your necklace," he says. The two of us have never discussed Franticek, though I suppose that at some point, Mother must have filled Father in on the details of my brief romance.

I am so moved I can hardly speak. Father has given me back our house, the one I thought I might never see again.

Thirteen

A man rides by on a black bicycle and tips his hat. That is our cue. One, two, three. "Please, Uncle Rahm!" we call out in perfect unison. "No more sardines!"

It is June 23, 1944, the day we've spent so many months rehearsing for. There is not a cloud in the sky and the air is warm but not hot. A fat bee buzzes in my ear and then flies off. The Danish Red Cross commission couldn't have chosen a more perfect day to visit Theresienstadt.

I am standing with a group of other children near the corner of the main square, stiff smiles pasted on our faces. We've been arranged according to height, as if we are posing for a school photograph.

There is an unusual smell in the air: soap. We were allowed extra bathing privileges before this visit, and we were even issued a tiny bar of extra soap and a new outfit each. I am wearing a navy blue pleated skirt and a white blouse with a starched collar that makes my neck itch. The hem of the skirt is coming undone in one spot and the collar is a little yellow inside, so I know they aren't new. I try not to think of the girl who wore these clothes before me and where she is now. Even so, I hope I might be allowed to keep the skirt and blouse even after the commission's visit.

On my way over, I notice new street signs. What was once L1 has been renamed Lake Street. Lake Street? What a joke. There is no lake in Theresienstadt! There's not even enough water for all of us.

My heart skips a beat when I spot shiny new signs over the doors on one of the buildings. They are written in a neat square script that I recognize as Father's. One reads *Boys' school*; another, *Closed during the holidays*. So, those murals in the infirmary are not Father's only contribution to the Embellishment! I can't help feeling a little bit ashamed. They are just signs, but I know too, that they are also more than that. They're lies. Father is using his talent to tell lies. That can't be right.

There is no school in Theresienstadt and no such thing as a holiday. All that matters to the Nazis is tricking the Danish commission into thinking Theresienstadt really is a model camp. If the Nazis succeed with their charade, the Danes will make a glowing report to the international community, and the Nazis can complete their assault on European Jews.

Everywhere I look, prisoners are playing the parts we've been assigned. At the main kitchen, bakers in white hats are baking bread, and when the commissioner walks through the main square, a man passes with a cart of fresh vegetables. Fat yellow onions, perfect potatoes, stalks of pale green celery, and the greenest spinach I have ever seen. I try not to gawk, though it has been more than a year since I saw any vegetable besides a potato or, now and then, a turnip.

The Danish commissioner is tall and loose-limbed. The old woman says his name is Dr. Franz Hvass. He smiles brightly when he passes us. "Good morning, boys and girls," he says. At first, we don't know what to do. We've been instructed not to say a single word to any of the Danish visitors. But when Commandant Rahm gives us a thin-lipped smile, we understand we are to say good morning back: "Good morning, Herr Doktor."

Dr. Hvass turns to Commandant Rahm. "When I was a child, I didn't like sardines myself."

Rahm nods understandingly. "We like to give the children sardines because they're high in protein."

The boy standing next to me kicks my leg, but I am afraid to laugh. We have all been told what trouble we can get in if anything at all goes wrong today. "One false move from any of you dirty Jews," the Nazis warned us, "and as soon as the commission leaves, we'll shoot you and everyone in your family."

Of course I know what the boy who kicked me is thinking: That we have never seen a sardine at Theresienstadt, let alone tasted one. So we just stand there, smiling like wax dummies in a shop window.

There are even red geraniums. One big terracotta pot overflowing with the bright blooms. Just before the commissioner passes the corner where we are standing, a small boy rushes over with the flowerpot. And now that the commissioner is on his way elsewhere in the camp, the boy, out of breath from his errand, has scooped the flowerpot up and is delivering it to Dr. Hvass's next stop. This way, Dr. Hvass can be duped into believing Theresienstadt is full of flowerpots and happy, well-dressed children whose only complaint is that we have to eat so many sardines! Underneath the smile pasted on my face, I am seething with resentment and rage. I want to scream, but of course, I can't. And knowing that only makes me want to scream more.

If only there was some way to let Dr. Hvass know the truth: that we are being worked to death; that we are starving and living in foul, unsanitary conditions; and that we live in constant fear of being sent on the next transport. And that we are the lucky ones because we are still alive, still here in this hellhole that Commandant Rahm has dressed up for the day, like Cinderella gone to the ball.

Later in the day, those of us who don't look too sickly are invited to a special performance of a children's opera called *Brundibar*. It was composed before the war by a musician named Hans Krasa, now a prisoner in Theresienstadt.

Listening to the music almost makes me forget that, sitting in the audience next to Theo, we are part of a performance—a special show Commandant Rahm is putting on for the Danish commission.

The words to the opera are in Czech, so the Czech children in the audience laugh more than we do. Still, Theo and I manage to follow the story: A brother and sister need milk for their mother, who is ill. Desperate for money to buy the milk, the children try to sing with Brundibar, an organ grinder, but he chases them away.

A young and handsome Czech prisoner plays Brundibar. The best part is when he twitches his whiskers. We can't help giggling at that, but when Dr. Hvass claps his hands, I wish I could take back my giggles. I don't want to help fool Dr. Hvass into believing Theresienstadt is a fine place. My chest hurts when I think that I, too, have helped the Nazis' cause. In that way, I'm a little like Father.

Mother was working in the soup kitchen the day of the Danish commission's visit. The air, she tells us later, was heavy with the smell of meat and onions, rare delicacies that were brought into the camp for the commission's visit. Dr. Hvass peeked into one of the cauldrons and remarked on the pleasant odor. "How are things here?" he asked a young woman who worked with Mother.

All eyes—those of her fellow prisoners, as well as Commandant Rahm's and those of the other Nazi officials who were present—turned to the woman. Mother told us how the woman took a deep breath and met Dr. Hvass's eyes. "If you want to know how things are," she told him. "Look around. Be sure and look around." And then, she rolled her eyes.

Rolling her eyes like that was a very brave thing to do. It was also the closest anyone came to telling Dr. Hvass the truth. All the prisoners who were there hoped he would understand the woman's double message and why she rolled her eyes.

But Dr. Hvass just smiled like a puppet. "That's exactly why I've come," he said, shaking the woman's hand and not seeming to notice how bony her fingers were or how her fingernails were misshapen from fungus. "To have a good look around."

Just then, Mother said, three prisoners walked into the kitchen, singing a German song.

It turned out Dr. Hvass spoke some German and that the song was one of his favorites. And so he joined in. Then Rahm had started singing too.

If, when we heard about it later, the whole thing hadn't been so evil and twisted, we might have laughed. Instead we try to tell each other the Danish visit won't affect us. In fact, as Father says, the Embellishment may buy us time. And that night, for the first time since we came to Theresienstadt, there are two scraps of meat in our soup—though still not enough to require a knife. Those two scraps, I suppose, are a reward for our cooperation. If I weren't so hungry, I'd spit them right out.

The next morning, the countess hears Commandant Rahm whistling in the main square. The countess passes the news on to Mother and Frau Davidels. Soon the old woman is talking. Apparently, Rahm stopped whistling long enough to tell one of his underlings: "There's been an exciting development. The visit was such a success that now we're going to produce a film!"

~⚬~

On Monday morning, when I open the door to the diet kitchen, three women workers are gossiping by the sink. Usually, Monday morning gossip has to do with which couples were spotted going into which cubbyholes the day before, and which husbands or wives are being betrayed. But today, because of the way the women's backs are hunched and how close they are standing to each other, I know they are discussing more serious matters. Matters I'm not supposed to know about.

So I do what any self-respecting girl in my position would do: I listen in. The stories children aren't supposed to hear are always the most interesting.

"It's an absolute disgrace," one of the women hisses.

"The people involved in the Embellishment and now in this film are making it worse for all of us. They're prolonging the war by helping the Nazis spread their lies," another woman says. Then she spits into the sink to emphasize her disgust.

Of course, I think about Father. He helped with the Enbellishment. But then, didn't we all?

The third woman sighs. "Have you two heard what that numbskull Hvass wrote in his report?"

The other two haven't heard.

"He said the living conditions here were relatively good. Can you believe that, 'relatively good'?"

One of the women makes a snorting sound.

"At this rate," the first woman says, "the rest of the world will never do a thing to help us. We'll perish in this model city."

"If they don't ship us east first."

I know the Embellishment was a lie, but now, for the first time, I see that it may well have made things worse for all of us. Much worse. "Oh no," I say. I mean to stay quiet, but the words slip out. What the women are saying makes perfect sense. Father is wrong. There *was* harm in the Embellishment, and there will be more harm in the film Commandant Rahm is planning. If the rest of the world can be convinced that life for the prisoners in Theresienstadt is relatively good, they'll never intervene on our behalf. Or on behalf of the prisoners in other camps who have it even worse than us.

I've been a prisoner in Theresienstadt since April, 1943, more than two years now. But I have never felt more trapped than I do at this moment. There is nowhere to go. I shall never get out of this dreadful place. No one will ever come to my rescue!

The women turn to the door where I am standing. When they see it is me who has spoken, they get busy with their work. One sloshes water around in a bucket; another reaches for the scrub brushes. The third woman tightens her apron and tucks her hair behind her ears so it won't get in her way while she works.

I feel their eyes on me as I go to collect my scrub brush from the shelf by the sink.

"Her father's that Dutch artist. The bald one. Joseph Van Raalte. He is part of the Embellishment," one of the women mutters under her breath, but loud enough so I will hear her disapproval. "And now I've heard he's going to work on that godforsaken film."

The skin on my arms and legs begins to itch. Though I bathed about ten days ago, I feel filthy. Outside, and inside. My father is helping the Nazis carry out their evil plan. And I am benefiting from my father's situation. It's because of him that we have our own apartment. It's because of him that we haven't been shipped off on a transport. It's because of him that Commandant Rahm sent Opa to us.

I scratch my skin so hard I leave a trail of red fingernail marks along my arm. But that doesn't make the dirty feeling go away.

Father hasn't said much about the film, though he tells Petr Kien it won't be a standard documentary. Of course not, I want to shout when I hear the two of them talking. Documentary films are made to tell the truth; this is going to be a propaganda film. It will tell lies! And everybody knows it. Including Father—and me.

The Nazi high command in Berlin is so pleased with the results of the Danish Red Cross commission visit, they have decided to shoot a film about Theresienstadt. This way, they can show the whole world what a wonderful place we live in. The plan makes me feel sick. I ache all over everywhere and it isn't my muscles or my bones, it's my heart. The worst part is that there's nothing I can do about any of it.

A prisoner named Kurt Geron will direct the film. I've seen Herr Geron around the camp, a small round man with a dark head of hair and a wide mouth, a little like a clown's. He was a famous stage actor in Berlin and later an important film director. Mother gets a little stage struck in his presence. "I saw him in *Blue Angel* opposite Marlene Dietrich. He was wonderful," she tells me. "One day I'd like to ask him what Marlene Dietrich was like. As a person, I mean."

Of course, Geron didn't have much choice when Rahm ordered him to produce the film. Had he refused to go along with the Nazis' plan, Geron and his wife would have been sent on the next transport east. But when I see him sitting on his canvas chair with the word *Directeur* sewn in bold letters on the back, and telling people where to stand and sit so he can get the best shots, I know it isn't just a matter of following orders. I can tell Geron takes pleasure in his task. I know from the way his eyes are shining that he enjoys feeling important and having people to order around. He seems to have forgotten that he is helping the Nazis spread their lies.

The film already has a title: *The Fuhrer Gives a City to the Jews*. And Geron cannot make the film alone.

All of us will have to cooperate when the film crew is around. And before the final filming can begin, the Nazis will have to approve a series of set drawings, drawings that will detail, scene by scene, what the film will show.

And who is the only artist talented enough to handle this assignment?

Why, Father, of course.

The pit Father has dug for himself and us is getting deeper. First there was the mural, then the signs. And now there is this film. This sickening phony film! There are new lines on Father's forehead and his eyes are looking glassy. I try to console myself by thinking that at least Father does not seem to be taking the same pleasure Geron does in his task.

⁘⟿

It is bedtime. Opa has dozed off. So far, he isn't snoring, but that can change at any moment. I hear Mother in the bathroom, playing a game with Theo that she used to play with me.

"I'm mailing you," she tells Theo in a teasing voice. Then I hear her make a ripping sound that is meant to be the sound of the brown wrapping paper coming off the roll. "I'll need stamps," she adds, and then I hear her smacking her lips as she pretends to lick the backs of the imaginary stamps. For a moment, I close my eyes and try to pretend I am back in Broek and that Mother is playing the game with me. But my imagination is not strong enough tonight. I'm too sad, too angry and too confused. Father is doing what he must to keep us all alive, but there is a cost. How shall we be able to live with ourselves if this propaganda film helps prolong the war and brings about the deaths of more innocent people?

"Where shall I mail you to tonight?" Mother asks Theo. "Paris? New York, perhaps? We've never been to New York. They say it's a grand city with buildings that reach to the sky."

At first, Theo doesn't say a thing. He is considering his answer. "Broek," he says at last. "Send me home." I know exactly how Theo feels. I so want to go home. But I also know that if we ever do return home, everything will have changed. I will never see Father—or myself—in the same way. I tug at my necklace and study the tiny picture of Broek. But tonight it brings me little comfort.

Father is sitting on the bench, staring at nothing in particular, his eyes glassy. I can't hold things in anymore. I need to talk to Father. I need to tell him how I feel about what he's doing.

So I tap his shoulder, a little too hard. Father turns around. He looks surprised, as if I've awakened him from a dream.

"Do you *have* to do it?" I ask him.

"Do what, Anneke?"

Now it's my turn to be surprised. How can Father not know what I am talking about? It's all I've been thinking about these last months. I watch Father's face. He is scrunching his forehead. I think he knows.

I feel a little dizzy, as if the floorboards beneath us have shifted. I've been angry at Father. I've blamed him and Mother for not getting us out of Holland in time, but I have never questioned him before. Never acted as if I understood more than him. But now I feel as if I do. As if I see things Father simply refuses to see. Because he's too afraid.

"You know," I say, a little hesitantly at first, but my voice grows stronger as I speak. "Do you have to make those drawings for the movie?"

Part of me already knows the answer. Yes, Father has to make the drawings. Just like Geron has to make the movie. If they refuse, both risk being sent on the next transport, along with their families. Which means us. Me. But at the same time, Father must know what he is doing is terribly wrong. If only he would at least admit it!

When Father stands up, he towers over me. His blue eyes shine and his nostrils flare like a horse's. I get a sinking feeling in my legs. Perhaps I've gone too far. But I can't take back my question. It hangs between us in the air like the smell of something rotting.

"You haven't the right to ask me that, child!" Father says, his voice booming. "No right at all." Then he lifts his hand, and for a second, I think he is going to slap me. In all my life, neither Father nor Mother has ever lifted a hand against me. The floorboards feel as if they are shifting again, only more quickly now. I take a step

Monique Polak

back toward the wall. Father lets his hand drop back to his side; then he sits back down on the bench. The bench lists to one side. He is breathing hard.

I think about apologizing, but I don't. Because I'm not sorry.

No, I'm glad I've finally spoken up. Why won't Father do the same? Why won't he tell the Nazis he won't draw lies? But already, I know the answer. He can't tell them anything. He can't speak up to them the way I've just spoken up to him. If he does, he risks everything. Everything!

As I try to settle on my mattress, I feel my heart pump in my chest. My temples throb. But it isn't a bad feeling. That's because, for the first time since Franticek and Hannelore left Theresienstadt, I feel a little bit alive again.

My sadness isn't gone. But at this very moment, it seems as if my fiery red anger has somehow burned the old sadness to ashes.

There are people who sneer when the film crew passes with its cameras and tripods and ladders and lights. Kurt Geron barks orders: "A little to the left! No, no a little more! Now there's too much sun in your eyes! Haven't you heard a single thing I've said?"

People whisper that Geron's big belly looks even bigger now that it is swollen with pride. "Perhaps Herr

Directeur has been eating *wienershnitzel* with his good friend the commandant," someone adds.

Several cameramen have been assigned to work with Geron, including a Czech Christian who was hired by Commandant Rahm for the project. And Father is usually hovering somewhere nearby with his sketchbook, comparing the scenes Geron is shooting with the ones in the sketchbook Commandant Rahm approved.

Geron and his crew film children playing in the newly constructed playground. Of course Geron is fussy about which children can appear in his film. "They have to look Jewish—and robust," I hear him say when he is rounding up children for that scene.

"Not her," he says, when he sees me. "Too blond and too bony."

Of course, there are few robust-looking people in Theresienstadt. When a woman suggests that if we children had a little more to eat we might look stronger, Geron pretends not to hear.

That is when I realize that though Geron is directing the film, he, too, is playing a role. He's been cast as the great film director. In that way, he is as much a puppet as the rest of us. The thought makes me feel angry with Geron and sorry for him, all at the same time. It's how I feel toward Father.

It is decided that a concert, performed by an orchestra of prisoners, will make another fine scene in the film. After all, what better way is there to show the world that the population of Theresienstadt is exposed to high culture?

Geron has asked Father and Mother to sit in the audience. Because he plans to seat them near the front of the café where the scene will be filmed, they'll have to wear their best clothes.

Mother pinches her cheeks to make it look as if she's applied rouge. Father dusts off his coat collar. "You and Theo and your opa must come too—to hear the music," he tells me the evening of the concert.

"I don't enjoy pretend concerts," I mutter under my breath.

Father polishes his eyeglasses. When he speaks, he doesn't lift his eyes to look at me. "You know," he says in a quiet voice, "on some level, all art is pretend. You should consider that, Anneke."

I don't feel like considering it. "It's still dishonest."

"Anneke." The sound of Father's voice tells me he thinks I have gone too far. He wants me to apologize. But I don't. I won't.

In the end, I go to the concert, but not for Father. I go for Opa, who is convinced that listening to music will take our minds off how hungry we are. We have to drag Theo away from his soccer game.

The three of us stand off to the side of the room since Geron doesn't want children or old people in this part of the movie.

"Listen to the music," Opa whispers, moving his finger in the air as if he is the one conducting.

But I can't listen. I can only watch Father and Mother, sitting side by side in the audience, their necks a little too straight, their faces a little too concentrated on the performance. When the camera lands on them, their faces tighten.

"Take two!" Geron shouts, and the musicians lay down their instruments on the floor beside them.

Father and Mother eye each other nervously. The camera was on them when Geron called for the second take. I can see they are worried they have done something wrong. And by now, Geron is known for having a temper when the filming doesn't go according to plan.

But Geron doesn't yell at Father and Mother. He yells at all of us, his voice ricocheting off the walls like gunfire. "This is all wrong!" he shouts. "All wrong! You people have to cooperate to make this film a success. You have to do something about the expression in your eyes! For God's sake, it looks as if you're all dead behind those eyes!"

It is a problem that even with all his shouting and carrying on, the great director cannot fix.

Fourteen

"I won't be long," Opa tells me. "I'm just going outside to empty the pot." My throat is too sore for arguing. Mother insisted I stay home from work. Rather than going all the way to the latrine, she has suggested I pee in a tin saucepot she found at the store. And now, probably because the day is so hot and humid, the sharp smell of my pee seems to take over the whole apartment. I can't blame Opa for wanting to empty the pot.

When someone raps at the door, my first thought is that something bad has happened to Opa. Perhaps he fell on the cobblestone street and hurt his head. I can already picture the bloody gash on the middle of his forehead. Who will bring him to the infirmary? So I open the door without even bothering to ask who is there.

When I gasp, the pain in my throat gets even worse. Three Nazis soldiers in gray uniforms and black boots push their way through the narrow doorframe. One kicks the wall, leaving behind an angry scuffmark.

"Is this the quarters of the artist Joseph Van Raalte?" the first soldier barks. Before I can open my mouth to say yes, the other two have already begun to turn the apartment upside down. One kicks over the mattresses, the other brushes his hands across the kitchen shelf. Mother's sugar bowl falls to the floor, breaking into a hundred pieces. My body shakes with fear. Even my fingers are trembling. If this is how they treat our things, what might they do to me?

I feel the soldier who seems to be in charge eyeing me, and I wish I was properly dressed and not in my torn flannel nightgown. I try to fasten the buttons near the collar. "To your knowledge," he asks, "does Joseph Van Raalte have any drawings in this apartment?"

"N-no," I stammer, "not to my knowledge."

I know Father sometimes keeps drawings he plans to sell on the black market beneath the mattress he and Mother share, but the officers have already looked there and found nothing. Then I remember the drawing Petr Kien made of me. Father stores it in his suitcase for safe-keeping. "Th-there's a sketch of Petr Kien's. In Father's suitcase. It was a g-gift," I manage to say. My lips feel stiff and it's hard to form the words.

"Show us," the first soldier says. He stands, with his hands on his hips, while I drag the suitcase out from behind the bathroom door. My arms feel weak.

"Have you ever heard of a man named Strass?" the officer asks.

My hands tremble as I lay the suitcase on my mattress. "The name Strass means nothing to me," I whisper.

"He's some Bohemian Jew, who, before the war, collected art. Apparently the dirty Jew is still collecting, and some of the art he has depicts conditions here as less than ideal." The soldier laughs. "That Strass is a no good moneymaking meddler, like all you Jews. Now open that suitcase!"

Though my head is spinning, things are beginning to make sense. I have heard of Herr Strass, and I am almost sure that Father *has* sold him sketches. I fumble with the buckle on the suitcase. Please God, I pray silently, don't let there be any of the kind of sketches these men are looking for inside.

"Open it! Now!" the soldier barks again.

When I open the suitcase, I feel the tension begin to drain out of me. There is only one sketch: Petr Kien's. Surely there is nothing criminal about it. The first soldier grabs the piece of cardboard, gives it a quick glance, then turns it over to check there is nothing incriminating on the other side. I half expect him to tear the sketch to shreds. But he doesn't. Instead he lets it fall to the floor, right near the heel of his boot. Then he steps on it, leaving the same scuffmark he's left on our wall.

"You let your father know," he says, his voice hard and angry, "that we are watching him." I can tell the soldier has noticed my trembling and it is only making him shout harder. But I can't stop. I'm so afraid.

"You let him know that any artist who has been producing what we deem inappropriate images will be punished. Severely!"

I am too frightened and too horrified to move. The drawings these soldiers are looking for tell the truth about Theresienstadt. That's why the soldiers are so angry! They're afraid that somehow, one day, people will see the drawings—and know the truth. But if the drawings are destroyed, no one will ever know the truth. There will be no point to all our suffering! It will be as if none of this ever happened. The thought makes me reach for my throat. People have to know! Otherwise, things like this—murders, lies, soldiers terrifying girls—will happen again. It's so unfair. I feel like falling to my knees and weeping. I feel like giving up. If no one ever learns the truth about Theresienstadt, what difference will it make if I do give up?

But the first soldier isn't yet through with me. He removes one of his thin black leather gloves and sticks his hand down the front of my nightgown. One of my buttons pops off and rolls along the floor, only stopping when it gets caught in a crack.

Then I feel his warm clammy hand squeeze my breast—hard. And then, he pinches my nipple. I want to cry out, but I don't. Something tells me that will only make him pinch me harder still. He has a wild leering look in his eyes.

No one has ever touched my breasts before, not even the doctor. When the soldier guffaws and pulls his hand out of my nightgown, I can still feel his touch. My nipple burns. "Not bad tits," the soldier says, "for a Jewess!" The other two join in his laughter.

I think I will vomit. Only my stomach is too empty for that.

When the soldiers leave, I try to tidy up the apartment, but I can't figure out where to start. With the mattress or the bits of sugar bowl? My mind's not working right. My nipple is so sore. I can still hear the soldier shouting at me!

"Oh my God, child," Opa says when he comes back and sees the mess. "What's happened here?"

By now, I am picking up what is left of Mother's sugar bowl from the floor. Already there are a few small cuts on my palms, but I don't care. I don't feel the cuts. It's as if my body's gone numb.

I tell Opa what the Nazis were looking for, but I leave out the part about my nightgown. I'm too ashamed to discuss such things with an old man. Nor can I imagine ever telling Mother. What would she think of me? If only I'd been well enough to go to work. If only I'd buttoned up my nightgown to the top. No, I know what I have to do: I must pretend it never happened. It will be easier that way.

"Here," Opa says, handing me a bit of rag, "use this to collect the shards. So you won't hurt your hands." Then he picks up Petr Kien's sketch and blows on it hard so some of the dust from the soldier's footprint disappears. Carefully, as if he thinks the sketch is something very valuable, he lays it back in the suitcase.

That is when I notice the other drawing. It is caught behind the felt-covered divider meant to

separate shoes from clothing. My heart thumps hard
in my chest as I take the drawing out and study it.
The sheet is divided into two parts: on the left, a
Nazi officer strides down a wide empty lane, a brief-
case dangling from one of his hands; on the right is
a thick throng of Jews, their shoulders hunched as
they struggle to move forward on their side of the
street. The picture captures how certain lanes in
Theresienstadt are reserved for the Nazis and how we
Jews are herded together like cattle.

I know Father made this drawing. Although he hasn't
signed it, I recognize his small, neat lines and the way he
likes to draw people from behind. I also know this is
precisely the kind of drawing those Nazi officers were
searching for.

For the first time I understand that though Father
often draws exactly what the Nazis tell him to draw,
there must be other times, times I've never known about
until now, when Father draws the truth. He must think it
would be too dangerous for me to know about all this.

So not all art is pretend.

Opa's hands are shaking. Like me, he understands
how dangerous this drawing is. "We need to destroy
it—burn it—in case they come back and search the
apartment again," he whispers.

I shake my head no. The drawing is too precious.
Not only because it tells the truth about Theresienstadt,
but also because it has helped me learn the whole truth
about Father.

I wedge the drawing back behind the felt-covered divider. No one will find it there.

.:σ⁓

The next day, nothing Mother says can keep me home. The memory of the three Nazis storming into the apartment, and of the one grabbing my breast, is too strong. I've wiped and wiped until the footprint came off the wall, but when I pulled my nightgown over my head, I saw blue marks across my left breast: the officer's paw print. Though I know it wasn't my fault, I feel ashamed. If only I'd gotten dressed yesterday morning.

All day, I try not to think about what happened. Only it isn't so easy to do. No matter how hard I scrub, my mind keeps landing on the memory.

At the end of the day, when I go back to the apartment, I feel more tired than I have ever felt. Not just because my throat aches and I've worked hard and eaten so little, but also because I've been fighting with myself all day, trying to control my thoughts. If only I can get a little sleep. Maybe then, I'll feel stronger tomorrow. And perhaps by then, the ugly blue paw print will begin to fade.

But I have not seen the last of the Nazi soldier who left his mark on me. When I walk into the apartment, Father is sitting on the bench, shifting nervously. I see shiny black boots, and my legs go weak. A Nazi is standing over Father, interrogating him, rattling off questions in quick succession.

I recognize the angry voice. It is the same Nazi who shoved his hand inside my nightgown. He sees me come in. When he winks, the sick feeling in my stomach returns.

My first impulse is to hide in the bathroom. But what if Father needs me? So I hurry to the corner of the room where Mother and Opa are huddled. I am glad it is still light outside. Theo will not be home during the interrogation.

By now, we've all heard that last night, Herr Strass and his wife were badly beaten. Strass's nose is broken and the wife can barely see out of one of her eyes. Nazis, perhaps the same three who came to our apartment, found a stash of food and drawings beneath Strass's mattress. But what upset them most was the news that photographs of a series of drawings depicting the terrible conditions at Theresienstadt were recently published in a Swiss newspaper. The Nazis are convinced it was Strass who smuggled the drawings out of the camp.

"Have you ever made a drawing depicting Theresienstadt in an unfavorable light?" the Nazi asks.

When Father looks into the Nazi's eyes and speaks in a calm even voice, I am shocked that he can lie so easily. "No, I haven't."

"Do you know of anybody who has ever made such a drawing?" the Nazi asks.

"No, I don't."

The soldier's eyes take on a strange glimmer. Opa shuts his eyes. I watch in horror as the Nazi's gloved hand forms a tight fist and he strikes Father—right in the mouth. Blood spurts from Father's lips, but he doesn't utter a sound. The only noise comes from Mother, who is whimpering. I squeeze her hand hard to make her stop. If you show any sign of weakness, the Nazis become even crueler.

When the Nazi removes his gloves, I have to suck in my breath so I will not be the one to whimper at the sight of his stubby fingers. My left breast throbs. He reaches inside a brown envelope he has tossed on my mattress. "What can you tell me about this drawing?" he asks Father.

This time Father flinches. I lean forward a little so I can see the drawing. Mercifully, it isn't one of Father's. This is a charcoal sketch with more black in it than white. Though I've never seen it before, there is something familiar about its style: the hatched lines, the attention to detail. I'm almost certain it was done by Norbert Troller, another artist in Father's studio.

No wonder Father is flinching. Mother must realize it too, because I feel her body suddenly go rigid.

Troller has covered every millimeter of the sheet with faces—thin, pale, anguished faces. And then I understand what scene he wanted to capture: the night of the census count.

Father uses the back of his hand to wipe the blood from his lip. "I recognize that drawing," he says.

My heart sinks. How can Father betray his colleague?

Father goes on, his voice as calm and even as before. "It was done by the artist Henk Van Gelder. A fellow Dutchman. He and his wife were transported east several months ago."

"Very well," the Nazi says. Then, as if for good measure, he gives Father a final punch, this one in the ribs.

Fifteen

For about two weeks, we hear nothing further about what is being called the Painters' Affair. Frau Strass's vision returns, though when her husband's nose heals it has a new bump on the bridge. The bruise on Father's abdomen fades to yellow before it disappears altogether. His lip, however, like Herr Strass's nose, will never be the same. There is a black blood spot in the middle of his upper lip. Mother says it gives him character. I know that for me, the blood spot will always remind me that Father has more courage than I gave him credit for.

Everyone in the studio where Father works hopes the Painters' Affair has simply faded from the Nazis' consciousness. It is rumored the Nazis have begun to face setbacks in their campaign to conquer Europe. Perhaps they are too busy worrying about the battlefield to concern themselves with the artists of Theresienstadt.

But, in the end, that isn't how it goes. True to form, the Nazis, so meticulous about keeping records, remember the Painters' Affair. But like tigers, they stalk their prey, and are only waiting for the right moment to pounce.

And so, on a steamy July morning, they come to the studio and round up five artists. Not Father, nor Norbert Troller, but nearly all the others, including Petr Kien. They have already come for Herr Strass and his wife. Thank goodness there is no evidence to incriminate Father.

"We have proof you five were involved in disseminating incriminating images," the Nazi in charge of the operation says.

Father tells us later how one of the artists cried out that all they did was draw the truth. The comment earned him such a hard blow across the head the man fell to the ground.

At lunch that day, the painters are taken away on a small truck. Those of us who can, come out to say goodbye. I go to stand by Father, whom I spotted watching from a doorway. One of the artists on the truck is Fritz Taussig, who goes by the name Fritta. Father points to a small dark-haired boy waving from the crowd. "That's Tomicek, Fritta's boy," he tells me, choking on his words. "He's only four."

"At least they're not sending them east," someone calls out when the driver puts the truck into gear and drives off.

"The Little Fortress is as bad as the east," someone calls back.

"Maybe worse," another voice adds.

The words themselves don't sound ominous. A little fortress might be a child's toy, like a cardboard castle or a wooden soldier. "Have you heard what happened to Otto Ungar's right hand?" Gizela asks when we meet at the washing fountain. The humidity makes her hair even frizzier than usual. "The old woman says the Nazis have mutilated Ungar's hand…so that he'll never paint again."

I can tell Gizela wants to be my friend. But I don't have the heart for friendship. I am too upset by the news of what the Nazis have done to Otto Ungar. Besides, talking with Gizela only reminds me of how much I miss Hannelore.

That night, as I am preparing for bed, I can't take my eyes off Father's hands. I know it could have been him. Had the Nazis found that other drawing, Father would be in the Little Fortress tonight. The thought prevents me from sleeping.

The next day after work, Gizela is waiting for me outside our apartment. She whispers that there is another rooftop we can visit. This one, she says, will allow us to peek at the Little Fortress. I can't say no. Though part of me wishes I could forget all about the Little Fortress, another part, a bigger part, wants to know…needs to know…the truth. Even if the truth is ugly.

But I am not prepared for how ugly the truth turns out to be.

Gizela and I are the only two who go. This rooftop is on a smaller building, with a staircase so narrow we can only climb it one at a time. "If the Nazis find out we can see the Little Fortress they'll kill us," says Gizela. One of the reasons I don't feel that comfortable with Gizela is that her frank way of speaking can be a little off-putting. But perhaps Gizela is right.

Because I don't fancy the idea of being killed, I am the one who suggests we lie on our bellies. From where we are, we can just see the Little Fortress, a brick star-shaped building surrounded by ramparts. It was designed to look like a miniature Theresienstadt. "I'd rather be dead than living there," Gizela says, her voice raspy.

We've heard that the artists who were arrested are being used as forced labor, made to dig in a limestone quarry in Litomerice, about a half hour's drive from Theresienstadt. "It's backbreaking work," I heard Father tell Mother, "but at least they're still alive."

Gizela and I watch as a truck, the same truck that took the artists away, stops in front of the Little Fortress. A group of men hobble out of the truck. I think I recognize Fritta's dark hair, so like his son's. Even from our perch, we can hear the tinny echo of the Nazi soldiers shouting, "*Raus! Raus!*"

We think the prisoners will be led inside. But it soon becomes clear the Nazis are not yet done with them. Someone shouts an order in German and next thing we know, the men who got off the truck are herded through a narrow passageway and into a grim-looking courtyard.

There, they are made to form a line and perform some bizarre sort of calisthenics, flapping their arms like giant birds and jumping up and down. Or at least trying to.

One prisoner, exhausted no doubt from his exertions at the quarry, falls to the ground. Like snakes, Gizela and I slither to the edge of the roof for a better view.

A Nazi soldier takes a bucket of water and throws it over the man lying on the ground. Though I am lying on the roof, it as if I can feel the water too. The water makes a brown puddle on the ground, but it fails to revive the prisoner.

The other prisoners seem to understand they cannot go to the man's rescue. Instead they continue with their sorry calisthenics, only now their arms flail about more and one nearly loses his footing. It breaks my heart to imagine how trapped and helpless they must feel right now.

The Nazi who dumped the bucket of water on the prisoner, approaches his body on the ground and kicks it. Once, hard, and then a second time, harder still. But the man on the ground does not get up.

I groan. Gizela sucks in her breath. I know no matter how long I live, I shall never forget this scene. I'm beginning to realize that though it is difficult for me to remember the good times—for instance, our life in Broek before the war—the bad times have become impossible to forget. They are now as much a part of me as my skin.

Gizela throws her arm over my back. "He's better off dead," she mutters.

The other painters don't remain long at the Little Fortress. They are shipped out on the next transport, so thin and battered-looking, they are almost unrecognizable. People think it best not to let Tomicek come to the train to see his father off.

Later we get one small bit of good news about the painters. Miraculously, a postcard arrives in Theresienstadt. Mail is rare and when it does come, it is so heavily censored that when you receive it, there are more heavy black lines than words on a page. Sometimes, people devise complicated codes to convey their messages.

This postcard comes from a place called Buchenwald, a concentration camp people say is near the German city of Weimar. The sender reports having seen the artist Otto Ungar. The card read: "Saw O.U. doing a charcoal sketch."

Has Ungar learned to draw with his other hand, or has he found a way to draw with the mutilated hand? Either way, it helps to think that though the Nazis broke Ungar's bones, they were not able to break his spirit.

Fall comes early to Theresienstadt in 1944. By October, the countryside has turned brownish yellow, and the nights have grown chilly. My blue sweater is wearing thin at the elbows. When it is announced one morning that all children under the age of sixteen must report to the Magdeburg Kaserne by seven o'clock, we are delighted to have the morning off from work. Our parents are less impressed. "I don't like the idea," I hear Mother tell Father.

"Keep a close eye on Theo," Father whispers to me when he says good-bye, kissing the tops of our heads.

Mother walks us to the corner of Backergasse Street. "Hello," she says, giving us each a long squeeze. After Theo's name appeared on the transport list, Mother came up with a new habit of saying "hello" instead of "good-bye." I suppose good-byes have become too painful for Mother. Her new habit never fails to make Theo laugh.

Hundreds of children are already congregated in front of the Magdeburg Kaserne. A Nazi officer shouts orders through a bullhorn. When I feel how cold Theo's hand is, I pull him closer and put his hand in my pocket.

"You will form a line that will stretch from in front of this barracks to the shores of the Eger River," the voice on the bullhorn announces. "Each of you will take the small cardboard box handed to you, then pass it on to the child at your left. The boxes contain materials for road paving. You are not—I repeat, you are not to speak to one another during this exercise."

The word "exercise" makes me think of the way the Nazis forced the painters to do calisthenics outside the Little Fortress. I shudder at the memory. It's one more awful image I now have to carry with me, like a satchel that's too heavy.

Someone tugs at my elbow. It is Gizela. She puts her finger to her lips to remind me not to speak, but her eyes are full of mischief. When I wave back, she comes to stand near us.

"Spread out so you are precisely one arm's length from each other," the voice commands. We do as we are told, and then, for about fifteen minutes, we wait in silence. By now, of course, we are accustomed to waiting. Theo, who is now too far away from me to put his hands in my pocket, blows on them to keep them warm.

At last there is a rustling at the front of the line. In the distance, I can see the children standing there have begun passing down the boxes. The boxes are long and narrow, only a little fatter than the boxes Opa used to pack ties in at his store in Zutphen. Soon, things begin to move so quickly we have no time to talk, even were we allowed to.

I take a cardboard box from Theo and pass it to Gizela. The moment that is done, I turn back to Theo, who is waiting with another box. I shift from right to left so often I grow dizzy. I try keeping count of the boxes, but there are too many and they come and go too quickly.

Of course, we are all wondering the same thing: Why do the Nazis want to dump road paving materials into the Eger River? Our assembly line slows down when something falls out of one of the boxes, and a boy stops to pick it up from the ground. "It's a tooth," we hear him say. "Imagine what a road paved with teeth would look like!"

Those of us who are old enough to read have already noticed words on the outsides of the boxes. Family names. Jewish family names written in bold black letters on neat white labels: Echenberg. Fleischmann. Friedman. Groenfeld.

The children standing closest to the riverbank confirm what the rest of us suspect. The cardboard boxes contain ashes. Powdery gray human ashes.

There are no terrible machines to gas people to death in Theresienstadt, but there are crematoria to dispose of corpses by burning them to ashes. The Nazis want to destroy the evidence: the ashes are proof that thousands of prisoners have died and been cremated here. And we are helping the Nazis dispose of the evidence.

Raisevitz. Stein. Teitelbaum. Weiss.

A terrible desperation takes hold of me. I can't let this happen! But when another Nazi marches past where I am standing, I know I have no choice. I take another box from Theo. The thought that I am holding someone's remains makes me feel queasy.

Gizela tries to make a joke of it. "There goes Mr. Weiss," she says as she grabs the box with his name on it from my hands.

I laugh, but mostly because I don't know what else to do.

Sixteen

"Head back, child. All the way back."

I lean my head back as far as it will go. A spider is spinning a web on one of the rafters. How lucky he is to be a spider and not a girl with inflamed tonsils!

"I'm afraid we're going to have to remove that pretty necklace you have on. Now say *aah*."

I say *aah*. Then I shut my eyes tight. Even so, I can't stop picturing Dr. Hayek's long thin metal tongs and the way they gleam under the infirmary lights.

Dr. Hayek is taking out my tonsils. He's told Mother and Father the surgery cannot be postponed any longer. We all know what that means. I've been missing too many days of work. Since January, there have been more transports than ever from Theresienstadt. People speculate it is all part of the Nazis' housekeeping plan. Just as they wanted to dispose of the ashes of those who perished in the camp, they are now determined to dispose of as many inmates as possible. Lately, sickly prisoners have been the first to go.

"The operation will be painful," Dr. Hayek tells me, "but once it's over and you've had a little time to recover, you'll be as good as new. And no more sore throats." I've had a sore throat for so long it is hard to imagine feeling well.

In Amsterdam, I would have had an anesthetic to numb my throat during the surgery. But in the Thereisenstadt infirmaries, there is no such thing. Even prisoners whose limbs have grown gangrenous and need to be amputated are operated on without anesthetic. When I think of them, I know I shouldn't complain about a troublesome pair of glands on either side of my throat.

Mother and Father bring me to the infirmary, but they can't stay with me. Neither of them can afford to be away from their work. So now I am alone with Dr. Hayek, a Czech Jew with a kindly face and bags so heavy under his eyes it is a wonder no one tried to search them at the *Schleuse*.

Dr. Hayek has a habit of laughing at his own bad jokes. "Do you know what we call this instrument?" he asks when I sit down on the hard chair in the little operating room.

I shake my head. "A guillotine!" he says, chuckling so hard the bags under his eyes wobble.

The word "guillotine" makes me shiver. I remember how Marie Antoinette, the beautiful Austrian princess, daughter of the empress after whom Theresienstadt was named, died on the guillotine.

I hear Dr. Hayek shuffling next to me, then washing his hands in the small sink. "The actual procedure will only take three or four minutes. I'm going to reach in with my guillotine, take hold of your tonsils and remove them. All in one fell swoop."

I clutch the sides of my chair. Why does Dr. Hayek have to keep saying the word "guillotine"?

When Dr. Hayek puts his instrument into my mouth, I gag. "Anneke," he says, sounding more like a school-teacher than a doctor, "you have to cooperate. The sooner we get this procedure over with, the better."

And so, though I want to gag, I don't let myself. Instead I clutch the chair so hard my nails dig into the wooden arms. I can feel my face getting hot as the long sharp end of the guillotine slides down the middle of my throat. The pain comes a moment later. A sharp searing pain—more terrible than anything I've ever felt before. I see a flashing silver light and then, just like that, I feel my mind leap out of my body. It flies off somewhere overhead, high, high up, past the rafters and the spider web, while my body remains seated in the infirmary chair.

It is Dr. Hayek's laughter that brings my mind back to my body. "I've never seen such tonsils," he cackles. "These are twice the size of normal tonsils. If I were a fisherman, I'd call this a good catch. A wonderful catch—the catch of the day!" That makes him laugh all over again. Only the sound seems to be coming from very far away.

Dr. Hayek pats my shoulder. "There, there, Anneke," he says. "All done. Would you like to meet your tonsils?"

I want to say no, thank you very much, I have no interest in meeting my tonsils, or anybody else's for that matter, but no words come out. My throat throbs as if, during the surgery, my heart had changed locations.

But I manage to open my eyes and when I do, I see Dr. Hayek with his guillotine. His eyes are shining. Hanging from the bottom of the guillotine are the ugliest things I have ever seen. Long and pinkish red, my tonsils have spots of white pus all over them.

I shut my eyes even more tightly than during the operation. At some point, Dr. Hayek must have helped me up from the chair, because when I wake up, I am lying in a cot, my throat more sore than ever.

⁖⟡

"You have to drink. Dr. Hayek says there's a danger of dehydration," Mother is telling me. But I can't sit up, let alone drink.

There are new lines around Mother's eyes, and I feel guilty for making her worry. But when I try to lift my head, my shoulders slump back on the mattress.

"She may not be ready yet to take water," a soft voice says. The voice belongs to a woman, though I can't see her. But someone, probably the woman, pries open the window and a gust of freezing air blows into the little room. A moment later, Mother is hovering over me with a blanket.

"Let her try this," the woman's voice says.

Strange hands pass me a chipped bowl. Inside is something frozen and green. "It's soup," the voice says, handing me a spoon. "I left it out on the windowsill for you."

I scrape at the frozen soup. Though the spoon is badly bent, it does the trick. Soon I loosen a few green slivers. It is pea soup. And when the frozen slivers touch the sides of my throat I think how I've never tasted anything quite so delicious.

"You're very kind," Mother tells the woman.

"I do what I can to help," the woman says. Now I can see her. She has straight dark hair that falls to her shoulders. It is Franticek's girlfriend.

··☞

Her name is Berta. During the four days I spend recuperating in the infirmary, she often looks in on me. Though Berta is part of the cleaning crew in the infirmary, she does what she can for the young patients, making us more comfortable on our cots, bringing fresh water when it is available and comforting those who have no parents to visit them.

On the second afternoon, I awaken to find Berta sitting on the edge of my bed, studying my face. "He loved you," she whispers.

Of course, I know she means Franticek. I must be getting stronger, because now, when I try to sit up, I don't topple over. I straighten my back and return Berta's look. Though her face is sweaty and her hands are raw and red, there is no question that she is a beautiful woman. A grown woman, one with whom I know I can't compare. I look down at my own bony, ill-shaped body and I hate her.

"You didn't mean a thing to him," I say.

Berta nods.

I don't know why I want so much to hurt her.

She turns to the window. "You're probably right," she whispers. "After all, he gave you the necklace."

Dr. Hayek kept Franticek's gift safe, and yesterday Mother tied it back around my neck.

I stroke the piece of leather.

⚬

The next day, while Berta sweeps around my mattress, I ask about her husband. "Don't you care for him?"

Berta stops sweeping and leans on her broom. "I used to care for him very much," she tells me, "but the war changed everything between us."

She tells me her husband is a Christian. When they first fell in love, the difference in their religions meant nothing. But later, when the Nazis came to power in Czechoslovakia, he turned on her. "He called me a dirty Jew and accused me of ruining his life. But when the

Nazis rounded up the Jews in our town, they took him too. 'If you're married to a Jew, why then, you're also polluted!' the Nazis told him."

"Oh, Berta, I'm so sorry."

"That wasn't the worst of it." When Berta resumes her sweeping, I know she doesn't want to tell me more.

But I feel as if I need to know. "What was the worst of it?" I venture.

Berta closes her eyes and shakes her head. "The worst...," she says, hesitating for a few moments before she can go on, "were the beatings. He used to beat me and the boys also." When she reaches for my hand, I let her take it.

I feel my heart opening to Berta. I can't hate someone who's lived through such misery.

"That was why I fell in love with Franticek, because he was gentle. Because he'd never have hurt a fly," Berta says. There are tears in her eyes.

"You were in love with Franticek?"

Berta nods. For the first time, I don't begrudge Berta for what she had with Franticek.

That night I have trouble falling asleep, perhaps because I've already spent so much of the day resting. Why is it, I wonder, that things always turn out to be so complicated?

Berta's not the monster I imagined. Nor is Father without courage. Even Commandant Rahm did one good thing.

How am I to make sense of all this?

It proves to be a hard winter, with more transports, each one larger than the last. Those of us who remain look at each other with a painful recognition. We are like the last chess pieces on the board. Will we survive until the end of the game?

According to the "old woman," the Nazis are continuing to sustain losses on the battlefront. But that doesn't necessarily help our situation. Life in Theresienstadt has become destabilized. The Nazis continue to bark orders, humiliate prisoners and organize transports to the east, but when they do so, we sometimes catch them looking over their shoulders, as if they know the end is near and they may have some explaining to do.

Like always, the old people whisper that the war is nearly over. Only now, I dare to believe them.

In April, when the air begins to warm up again, a representative from the International Red Cross comes to the camp. I am walking near the main square on the lane reserved for Jews when he takes leave of Commandant Rahm. I witness their stiff handshake outside the Nazi headquarters. Something appears to have been decided.

The visit gets the old woman's tongue wagging again. "The international community is going to do something at last," people say. Others are less hopeful. "The Red Cross didn't intervene to help us before. Why," they ask, "would they help us now?"

But exactly a week afterward, a bus pulls up at the front gates. It is white with large red crosses on each side. Then comes an announcement on the public address system: "All Danish prisoners have one hour to report to the main gates. With their satchels."

I can hardly believe the news. Surely, it bodes well for all of us.

Theo is collecting firewood near the gates when the bus drives off. "Commandant Rahm was there watching," Theo tells us that evening when we are picking the bugs off our blankets.

"What did Commandant Rahm say?" Opa wants to know.

"What did Commandant Rahm do?" Father asks.

Theo clears his throat. You can see he is enjoying the attention. "Commandant Rahm didn't say anything. He didn't do anything. He just stood there like a zombie."

✧

I hope the departure of the Danes bodes well for those of us who remain. But things get worse—far worse—before they begin to get better.

The very next afternoon a train arrives in Theresienstadt. There is no point in sending the people who get off to the *Schleuse* because it is clear they possess nothing of value. It is also clear from their greenish complexions, and the way they are doubled over, some with cramps, some because their heads ache too much for them to stand up straight, that these new inmates are ill.

"Keep as far away from them as you can," Berta warns when Mother and I meet her and her boys in the soup line. Then she drops her voice so the boys won't hear what she is about to say. "The newcomers have typhus. Dr. Hayek says the disease is highly contagious and that if we're not careful, the Nazis won't have to bother killing us."

Seventeen

The newcomers don't bring only contagion, they also bring news. The old woman says they have come from other camps, places like Auschwitz and Bergen-Belsen. Panic-stricken that the Russians and perhaps even the Americans are moving closer, the Nazis are trying desperately to empty the death camps.

The Council of Elders does what it can to ensure that those with the dreaded disease are kept in quarantine in a separate barracks. But typhus, a disease transmitted by lice, is so contagious it is almost impossible to prevent its spread. We are constantly on the lookout for its early signs: exhaustion, chills and a spotty rash.

When Theo wakes up two mornings later with red spots on his chest, Mother, whom I've never seen cry, even on our worst days in the camp, begins to wail. "You can't get sick now—not after we've been through so much," she tells Theo, making it sound as if he's caused the rash himself. But by evening, the rash disappears, and Mother calms down.

Father shakes his head. "Your mother is the strongest woman I have ever known," he tells me when Mother's back is turned. "But even strong women have their breaking point."

Of all of us, Opa seems to be faring the best. Because he was imprisoned in Bergen-Belsen, he recognizes some of his former bunkmates among those who stepped off the trains from the east. "My God," he calls out one evening after we've slurped down our soup. "There goes Igor Spivack! Spivack! Wait!"

It turns out Igor Spivack is nearly deaf (he was boxed on the ears by the Nazis for not shoveling quickly enough), so Opa sends me after him. I tap on the old man's shoulder. "Are you Igor Spivack? My grandfather is over there. He says he knows you from Bergen-Belsen."

When Spivack and Opa fall into each other's arms, all I can think about is that Spivack might be carrying the typhus bacteria. I lead the two of them to the nearest bench and take a few steps back, just in case. Of course, if Spivack infects Opa, I'll end up infected too, and then Mother and Father and Theo will also fall ill. Mother is right: Dying now, when we are so close to what we all hope is the end of the war—well, that would be too much to bear.

I watch Opa wipe his eyes as Spivack, a Rumanian Jew, tells him about their other bunkmates, nearly all of whom were gassed. "I still don't know why they spared me," Spivack says, sounding as if he thinks it would be better to be dead than a witness to all he's seen.

Afterward, Spivack turns in my direction. "There's something about you, something about the way you watch people," he says, shaking a wrinkled finger in the air, "that reminds me of a girl, a German girl about your age whom I knew in Bergen-Belsen. She and her family were hiding in Amsterdam when the Nazis rooted them out. Her name was Eva. She had a sister. Ilse was her name, I think."

I freeze in the spot where I am standing. Eva. My old friend from the Jewish Lyceum, the girl with the beautiful outfits and the dark eyes. "Where is she now?" I manage to ask.

"Dead. She and Ilse, both. Of typhus."

⚭

Even if the end of the war really is coming close, I begin to feel as if I want to give up. I've heard Mother and Father whisper about prisoners who have committed suicide in Theresienstadt: people who've hanged themselves, and a man who slit his wrist with glass from a broken windowpane. Before I came to Theresienstadt, I never understood why someone would take his own life. But I understand now: They simply wanted to put an end to the pain. Unbidden, a line from Heinrich Heine's poetry pops into my head: "My heart, my heart is heavy." Heine understood how I feel now. My heart is so heavy I can barely stay standing.

There has been so much pain, so much loss, I almost can't see the sense of living anymore. Franticek, Hannelore, and now Eva and Ilse, all gone. Gone! Vanished from the face of the Earth without a trace! And those are only the ones I cared for. What about all the others, the hundreds of thousands of others, perhaps even more than that—and all the people who cared for them? I feel as if our collective sorrow will leave us as bent and broken as the sickly souls who come on the cattle cars from Auschwitz and Bergen-Belsen. How will we ever find the strength to stand tall again? I don't think I have my mother's strength.

One March morning, I notice a purple crocus on my way to the diet kitchen. Bright and hardy-looking, it blooms on the side of the road, between two chipped cobblestones.

When I hear the sounds of a train chug-chugging into the camp, I groan. Please, I think, don't send us any more typhus-infected prisoners!

By the time I report to the diet kitchen, Frau Davidels has already heard the latest news. "This train isn't from the east, Anneke," she tells me. "It's from Holland."

"It is?"

Now I see why Opa was eager to see who came from Bergen-Belsen. It has been over a year since any Hollanders arrived in Theresienstadt. Perhaps these new arrivals will have information. Surely they will be able to tell us if the war really is coming to an end. "Can I go, Frau Davidels? Please!"

But when I get to the station, there is no one left except a woman carrying a pail of filthy water. "It was a small transport," she tells me. "Only about fifty of them. The train came from a town called Delft."

I haven't heard the word "Delft" in nearly two-and-a-half years. It makes me think of Mother's prized blue and white teapot, which was made in Delft.

"Where are they? At the *Schleuse*?"

The woman shrugs. "Where else? Even if the end of the war is round the corner, it hasn't made the Nazis any less greedy for our things."

But things have stopped mattering to me. What I really want is to see these people from my country. And hear their stories.

⁓⁓

Oom Edouard, Tante Cooi and Izabel are on the transport from Delft. Opa weeps with joy when he finds out. "At least we're all together now," he tells me. "Being together is the most important thing."

I am not so sure that is true.

Oom Edouard, Tante Cooi and Izabel are in a state of shock. Surely, they'd have been better off if they could have stayed in Amsterdam. Oom Edouard, a notary with many important connections in the city, was one of the last Jews in Amsterdam to be rounded up.

At least the three newcomers have us to show them around and explain how things work in Theresienstadt.

Izabel is horrified to learn we only have a chance to bathe once every three weeks. "What about your hair? How do you keep it clean?" she asks me, her eyes pooling with tears.

"I don't." I'm suddenly aware of how stringy my own hair feels and how when I touch it, my fingers get greasy. Hair is just another thing that has stopped mattering to me.

Wait until Izabel finds out about the latrines, I think.

We are sitting on the stoop outside our apartment. Father, Mother, Oom Edouard and Tante Cooi are upstairs, catching up. A little boy with hair so blond it is almost white walks by and waves at Izabel. He can't be more than five. He looks so much like Theo when he was that age, it nearly takes my breath away. I suddenly remember Theo digging for worms behind our house in Broek.

"Can you come play?" the boy asks Izabel.

"I don't feel much like playing," she answers.

"What about your friend?"

"Neither of us feels like playing."

The boy shrugs.

Izabel tells me his name is Ronald Waterman. He and his parents were also on the transport from Delft.

The boy is too little to be out alone. "Ronald!" I call after him. "Wait for me! I'm Izabel's cousin—we can play."

When Ronald turns around, I notice his blue eyes have a touch of purple in them.

.:☞

"This is a very ugly place. Everything is gray," Ronald says. "No wonder everybody is so unhappy here."

"You're right about that," I tell him. It occurs to me I won't have to work very hard to make conversation with Ronald. The little boy seems always to have something or other to say.

"I've never seen so many sour faces," Ronald says.

It seems perfectly natural when he reaches for my hand. "You're more friendly than your cousin. If you ask me, she's a bit of a grouch."

I smile. "She's had a hard day."

"Me too. But I'm still friendly. Do you know how to skip?"

I haven't skipped in so long that when I do I can't help laughing. The Nazis have taken so much away from me, but they can't take everything.

It occurs to me that this little boy, who reminds me so much of my brother, is doing me good. Please, I think, hoping that God is listening, don't let anything bad happen to Ronald. Don't let him catch typhus. Don't let the Nazis ship him off to the east or hurt him in any way. Let him live to be a man.

And for the first time in many months, I feel a glimmer of hope for myself. If Ronald can live to be a man, well then, maybe I can live too. Maybe I'll survive this dreadful war. Maybe I'll be able to carry on, to begin a new life once the war is over. Maybe this grayness isn't all there is. Maybe I won't always be surrounded by these ugly ramparts that keep me trapped inside Theresienstadt.

"Soon you'll have to line up for your soup," I tell Ronald when we stop to catch our breath.

"I like soup," he tells me. "Especially Mother's *erwtensoep*. Before the war, she sometimes put sausage in it."

I don't have the heart to tell him about the watery lentil soup he'll have for dinner. "Maybe we can go for a skip again tomorrow," I say instead.

.·☌~

"No skipping just now. Walk straight and keep your head down," I whisper. There is a pair of Nazi soldiers walking up ahead.

"Why do I have to keep my head down?" Ronald asks, too loudly.

"Shh."

But the Nazis are too involved in their own conversation to pay any attention to us. We are close enough to hear what they are saying. "Rahm agrees with Eichmann that the Theresienstadt ghetto and its last inhabitants must be preserved, to show the world we haven't mistreated our prisoners," one of the soldiers says. Eichmann's name makes me shiver. He was the one who ordered some of the transports out of Theresienstadt.

"I'm against it," the second officer says, without bothering to lower his voice. "And there are many who agree with me: We should get rid of every last Jew while we can." His words make me shiver even more.

I try to steady my nerves by taking a few deep breaths. "Is something wrong, Anneke?" Ronald asks, looking up at me. The Nazis soldiers have disappeared around a corner, but their words still hang in the air. My body feels icy cold.

Ronald wrinkles his nose. "I smell smoke," he says.

I sniff the air. Ronald is right. Why didn't I notice the cloud of smoke directly over SS headquarters?

We have to pass there on our way to the children's barracks where Ronald is living. Tiny black cinders swirl in the air and one lands in Ronald's eye. He cries out from the pain. "Don't rub it," I say as I kneel down to inspect the eye. "Rubbing will only make it worse."

A scrap of charred paper lands on the cobblestone in front of me. I pick it up and hold it to the light. I can make out a few typed numbers and words. "12/3/1901, shoemaker, born in Brno, Czechoslovakia."

Later that night, I hear Father tell Mother that the Reich Central Security Office has ordered the destruction of every single file and index card in Theresienstadt. The Nazis emptied a water tank in the central courtyard and burned the documents inside the tank.

There will be no trace left of the Czech shoemaker.

I am too sad for words.

Eighteen

What is an empty freight train doing at the station, its doors wide open? No one has said anything about another transport.

Our mouths drop when we see the latest passengers preparing to take their leave of Theresienstadt. They are all, each and every one of them, Nazis! What can this mean? Where are they going?

Though they have proper suitcases, not rucksacks, and they wear shiny shoes and coats with brass buttons, they have something in common with the thousands whom we've already seen off at the station: an empty terrified look in their eyes. I'm glad it's *their* turn now to be terrified. Let them see what fear feels like!

So it has to be true: The Russians are coming, and the end of the war is near. The Nazis are fleeing back to Germany.

I think I see the soldier who squeezed my breast and beat Father. He is smaller than I remember, and I note with pleasure how his hands shake when he picks up his suitcase from the ground. I would like to shout at him, to let him know how much I hate him and how I hope he will pay for his sins, but Berta won't let me. "It's best not to provoke them," she says, lifting her chin toward the rifles hanging over the Nazis' shoulders.

They all leave on the train, except for Commandant Rahm and a handful of his men. When Rahm himself gets on the public address system and announces there will be a meeting at the café that was built during the Embellishment, we don't know what to think. What can he possibly have to say to us now?

A dark-haired boy races up the stairs to our apartment. "The watchmen are no longer in their stations!" he shouts excitedly. "The Russians are coming!"

No watchmen on guard in the tall towers that surround Theresienstadt, surveying our every move?

We could leave—walk out the front gates and begin our new lives right now. But we don't dare to leave. Instead we do as we are told and go to Rahm's meeting.

There are no more than two hundred of us. Frau Davidels says there are several hundred other prisoners still in the camp, lying in their sickbeds, too weak to attend. So this is what has become of the many thousands of prisoners who were sent to Theresienstadt.

Rahm clears his throat. His nose looks red and veiny. I wonder if he's been drinking. "Ladies and gentlemen," he begins.

There is a twitter in the audience. Someone laughs out loud. Others jab each other's elbows. These are things we'd never have dared do even a few days ago.

In the time I've known Rahm, he has called us many things, but never "ladies and gentlemen." He dabs at his forehead with a handkerchief that he takes out of his jacket pocket. "I want you to remember one thing," he says, "just one thing. And that's how lucky you have been. Remember always how the German Fatherland looked after you."

I turn first to my left, then my right. Everywhere I see thin, pale, broken faces. Someone coughs. Rahm is partly right. Compared to all those who have perished, we are indeed the lucky ones. But Rahm's Fatherland has not done a very good job of looking after us.

A youngish man stands up and jeers. Others sit in silence, astonished by what they've heard.

Without saying another word, Rahm turns his back on us and marches out of the café. His lackeys follow close behind. There is a truck waiting for them outside.

⁂

With no more Nazis in the camp, I'm not sure what to do next. It's a strange feeling. I've been following orders for so long I feel a little lost without someone telling me what to do. "Clean that cauldron!" "No talking in the soup line!" "Pass those cardboard boxes, dirty Jews!"

There is no sense reporting to work. On the other hand, we have to eat. And those who are ill require medical attention. So yes, there is much to do.

"Are we still prisoners?" Theo asks Father.

Father hesitates. "Of course not."

"Then why don't we go home?"

"Everything in its time."

Mother grabs my hand and kisses my fingers. "Come help me find food," she says. The diet kitchen is teeming with people who have the same idea. Someone tosses us an onion. I hold it to my chest. A whole yellow onion!

When we pass the Podmokly Kaserne, where the Nazi officers were billeted, I spot a long roll of what seems in the distance to be fabric. Bright yellow fabric, as bright as the sun, lying against the side of the building. "Should we take it?" I ask Mother. "Perhaps it can be used for bandages."

It is only when we are close enough to touch it that we realize what sort of fabric this is. Yellow stars. Rows and rows of them, with the German word *Jude*—Jew— inscribed beneath each one in heavy black letters. The bolt must weigh nearly as much as me, but even so, I manage to cart it back to our apartment. I'm still hungry, but my strength is coming back.

⁖

We hear the tanks before we see them. A low roar, growing steadily louder, then dozens and dozens of dusty tanks, followed by almost as many dusty cars. There are men on horseback, and there are cannons too. "Hurrah! It's Koniev's Fifth Army Guards!" voices call out. "They have come to liberate Theresienstadt!"

I want to be happy, but mostly I feel as if I am in a dream. Or as if I am just beginning to wake up from a terrifying nightmare.

Theo wants to go off with one of his soccer friends, to see the tanks up close. "Bring this to the soldiers," Mother says, handing him a cup of water. "They'll be thirsty on such a warm day."

When Theo comes back, his eyes are glowing. "Look what they gave me," he says breathlessly. Then he shows us what he is hiding behind his back: a German pistol. A Luger, but thank goodness, with no bullets inside.

Mother gasps, but Father laughs. His old throaty laugh, the one that starts in his belly. It is a sound I'd nearly forgotten.

Before the Russians came to Theresienstadt, I sometimes dreamt of what I'd do when I finally got my hands on a Nazi, or any German, for that matter. Aren't they all responsible, after all?

Sometimes my victim was the Nazi officer who'd thrust his sweaty hand inside my nightgown. In my dream, I pulled his hand away, called him a dog and told him to leave me alone. When he tried to hit Father, I tripped the Nazi from behind, and I laughed when he fell to the floor. Or sometimes I stared him in the face and spat at him, watching as my saliva dribbled down his chin.

Sometimes my victim was Commandant Rahm. In my dreams, I planned a special torture all for him. I did to him what he had ordered done to the artists. I sent him to work all day in the quarries, then forced him to do calisthenics until he collapsed. And then I kicked him until he was dead.

That dream was so real that when I woke up the muscles in my legs ached. As if I really had kicked him.

⁓

Theo and I will return to Holland by train. Dr. Hayek has examined us and pronounced us strong enough to make the journey home.

"We still have some business here, and your Opa needs to be a little stronger before he is ready to travel," Father explains. The Russians have set up a temporary office and are interviewing inmates in order to decide whether and how soon they can be released.

They have some questions for Father. They know about the other artists who died, and they want to know how he managed to survive.

"Can't we wait for you?" I ask Father.

"It's better this way. The Lunshofs will meet you in Haarlem. Mother and I will join you there. Don't worry so much, Anneke."

"I thought you always said the most important thing was to stay together."

"Not right now, Anneke."

"Will everything be all right?" I ask Father. I am watching his face.

Father nods. "Of course it will."

"But the Russians. They'll want to know..." I don't finish my sentence. But Father knows what I mean.

"I haven't done anything wrong," he says. "I did what I had to do. There was no choice."

And so, two days later, Theo and I board a train bound for Holland. This time, we have proper seats, and there is a bathroom in the next carriage. I wonder whether, like me, Theo is remembering our last train ride. But I don't ask, in case he isn't. I don't want to remind him of it. Right now, Theo has no one but me to look after him.

I gaze out the window at the bright green fields and the puffy clouds. The landscape still looks the same. But everything else has changed. Theo falls asleep. I try to sleep as well, but my mind is too awake. I keep seeing pictures of Theresienstadt and the people I've known there: Frau Davidels in her white bonnet, Hannelore the first time I saw her climb out of her cauldron, Franticek giving me his necklace, the Bialystok orphans dressed in rags, Berta watching over me at the infirmary.

Will my mind ever settle down or will these images stay with me until my dying day? I've left Theresienstadt, but it seems I've taken the place with me. I shake my head as if that will make the pictures go away. But it doesn't work. Now I see Ronald's purplish blue eyes.

Once we leave Czechoslovakia, we have to pass through Germany before we can reach Holland. The train screeches to a halt at the Bremen station. A girl with thick glasses is waiting on the platform. She gasps when she steps into our carriage.

She takes the seat closest to the door. I can see she is watching us, watching her. She crosses her legs. "*Guten tag*," she says in a quiet voice.

That is all she has to say.

"You're one of them, aren't you? A no-good Nazi!" one of the older boys in our carriage cries out. The boy sitting next to him leaps to his feet. The commotion wakes Theo. "What's going on?" he asks, rubbing his eyes.

One of the Dutch boys has got his hands on an ink pen. Was it also a gift from the Russians? If so, I think it is a much better gift than Theo's Luger, now safely stashed at the bottom of his rucksack. An ink pen can be used to make drawings or to write down stories. A gun is only good for scaring people—or worse.

The boy with the pen forces the German girl to her feet. "Turn around," he tells her. And then he uses the ink pen to draw a swastika on her back.

"I'm not a Nazi," the girl protests, her voice trembling.

"Of course you're a Nazi," her attacker says. "You *moffen* are all Nazis. Every last one of you! Now give me your shoes! Now!" The way he says it reminds me of the Nazi soldiers who came to our apartment looking for illegal art.

Whimpering, the girl unlaces her shoes. I did not notice them before, but now I see that they are black and scuffed. But unlike mine, they have no holes. I stare at them. Shoes without holes. I've forgotten what that looks like.

The boy sticks his nose inside one of the shoes. "They don't stink too bad," he says, laughing, "for *moffen* shoes!" Then he tosses the pair of shoes in my direction. "Here," he says, "a gift from the Fatherland."

The girl is sobbing now. Her shoulders shake. One of her white socks has a hole at the toe.

The shoes land in my lap. The boys return to their seats, calmer now that they have turned on the girl. The shoes will probably fit me. I could put them on, or I could go over and kick the girl. Like in my dream. But this is nothing like my dream.

When I get up, I know that now everyone in the car is watching me. I walk over to the girl and hand her back her shoes. "I don't want any gifts from the Fatherland," I say, loudly enough so everyone will hear.

⁖☞

When Anita Lunshof sees us she bursts into tears.

Theo looks confused. "Father said you'd be happy to see us."

"I am. It's just that, you look so..." Anita crouches down and gathers us in her arms.

Her husband, Jan, shifts from one foot to the other. "Let's get the two of you home—and into the bathtub."

Because the Lunshofs live in the center of Haarlem, we walk to their house. Theo and I visited Haarlem before the war, and though it isn't home to us, the Dutchness of the city—the fishing boats moored alongside the canal; the narrow, linked, brown brick houses; the white lace curtains in the windows; the bicycles parked in the lanes—feels familiar. I wish Father and Mother and Opa could be here too, so we could share the feeling of being back in our own country.

In the streets, people glance over their shoulders at Theo and me. Some point or whisper when they see us pass. Perhaps it is our old clothes or because we are so thin, but they seem to know where we've been. Will people always be able to tell?

"How would you like some bread with syrup for your dinner?" Anita Lunshof asks when we are seated at the wooden nook in her bright kitchen.

"I'd prefer *poffertjes*," Theo calls out. He hasn't forgotten the small pancakes Mother used to make as a special treat.

"I'm afraid it takes milk and eggs to make *poffertjes*," Anita says, "and we haven't had either of those things in ages."

"Bread with syrup sounds delicious," I say.

Our rucksacks disappear. Flore, the Lunshofs' housemaid must have whisked them to the backroom because soon I smell soap and a little later, I hear the creak of the wash line as Flore hangs out the clothes in the back garden.

When I can't eat any more bread with syrup, I go to look out the kitchen window. A black and white cat is lying on the grass, his belly exposed to the air. The wind is growing stronger; the clothes hanging on the line fill up like sails. That is when I see my cream silk dress, the one I wore when I was little and which I packed without Mother's knowledge. How could I have forgotten all about it? Mother must have found it and put it in my rucksack.

⋯o⌒

When I get up, I can hear the sounds of the household, and I realize I have slept late. Our laundry is neatly folded on a chair by the door.

"I need a hammer and nails," I tell Theo, who is sharing the guestroom with me.

"I saw a toolbox in the hallway."

When Theo returns with the box, I go straight to work, hammering six nails into the mahogany paneling. Three for me, three for Theo. I do my best to keep them in an even line. Now we have a place to hang our clothes.

There is a knock on the door. "Are you two sleepy-heads awake?" Anita Lunshof asks. "I thought I heard sounds coming from up here. Did you sleep well?"

Anita puts her hand to her mouth when she sees my handiwork. "Why in the world have you gone and hammered into the fine mahogany, Anneke?"

I didn't mean any harm. I take my silk dress and hang it carefully on the first nail.

Anita shakes her head. "Why, Anneke, we keep our clothes in a closet. Have you forgotten what a closet is for?"

I am too embarrassed to admit I have.

Nineteen

"*Y*ou are Anneke?"

The man is standing in front of me, but his voice echoes in my ears. The brass buttons on his jacket gleam, distracting me from his question. The buttons, the uniform, the shiny black boots and the man's sharp tone of voice all distract me. I feel the backs of my knees turn to jelly. My stomach churns.

Father pats my elbow, a quick warm pat that brings me back to reality. A pat that tells me everything is all right. The war is over. We are in The Hague in Holland, safely back in our own country. The nightmare is over.

Father has been summoned to the Dutch military headquarters to answer some more questions. In the end, he agreed to let me tag along. But he never said they might have questions for me.

"Anneke?" Father says, his voice not much louder than a whisper. He turns to the officer. "She's been through a lot," he tells him. "She's only sixteen."

I gulp. It will be easier if I look at the man's face—his clear blue eyes, his rosy cheeks—and not at the row of gleaming buttons. "Yes," I say, "I'm Anneke Van Raalte." There, that wasn't so hard.

The officer sits down behind his desk and reaches for his glasses. They have wire rims. Then he reaches into his pocket for a handkerchief and polishes the lenses. When he finally puts his glasses back on the edge of his nose, he looks like an owl. "Tell me where you spent the last two years, Anneke."

When I turn to look at Father, he nods his head.

I gulp again. "Theresienstadt," I say.

When the officer jots something in his note-book, his pen makes a scratching sound. Then he looks up at me again. "So you and your father survived Theresienstadt?"

"Yes, and also my mother and my brother, Theo, I mean Theodoor. And my opa too. We all survived."

The officer turns to Father. "I see," he says. "All five of you Jews survived?" He rubs his chin. "It's highly suspicious!"

I can feel my heart pounding under my blouse. I cannot let myself be frightened by a row of brass buttons or a pair of shiny black boots, even if they look like the kind of boots the Nazis wore. No, I have something important to say to this Dutch officer.

Besides, what can this man with his owl eyes do to me? I lost much in Theresienstadt: my innocence, my belief that all people were basically good. But now I have the heady sense that I have nothing left to lose. I don't need to be afraid ever again—of anybody.

I've witnessed terrible things I'll never forget, but I survived. Surely that means I can survive anything. Even this man's rude remarks. Imagine him saying it's "highly suspicious" that all five of us survived! The nerve of him. What can he possibly understand about what we've lived through?

I meet the officer's eye. "What do you mean exactly," I ask, "when you say it's 'highly suspicious' that our family survived Theresienstadt?"

"Anneke," Father whispers, "there's no sense in getting upset."

The officer shuffles some papers on his desk. Then he looks up at me again. "What I mean, young lady, is so few of you Jews survived, surely you did something, or perhaps your father did something, to ensure your safety."

So the officer knows about the drawings Father made for the Nazis!

When Father flinches, I pat his elbow.

I have always needed Father, even in Theresienstadt when I was most angry with him. But this is the first time I've ever had the feeling that Father may need me.

I keep my eyes on the officer. "Do you also know about Father's other drawings—the ones he hid—the ones that had they been discovered by the Nazis, Father would have been tortured...or killed?" Inside I'm a little shaky, but my voice is strong and steady. That gives me courage.

The officer jots something in his notebook.

But I still have more to say. "You're quite right.
Father kept us safe. He did whatever he had to do to
protect us, just as I hope you would do for your children." I notice some gray in the officer's hair, near his
temples. "And your grandchildren."

On our way out of the building, I tell Father I am
sorry.

Father's face is still painfully thin. "For what,
Anneke? For what?" I'm afraid he is about to cry.

This part is harder for me than standing up to the
Dutch officer. It's not that I've stopped questioning
what Father did to keep us alive. In fact I think no
matter how old I get, some part of me will always question what Father did to keep himself and us alive in
Theresienstadt.

But something important has changed. Now I understand that Father really had no choice. And I know that
he must live with that burden. Just as I shall live with it
until I take my last breath on Earth.

I'm sorry if I have made things even harder for
Father. But I couldn't help myself. I had to let him
know how I felt about what he was doing. I had to
stand up for what I believed was right. I suppose I had
to learn.

"I'm sorry for waiting too long to thank you."

Father smiles. "Oh, Anneke," he says, "you haven't
waited too long."

His eyes look silvery blue in the sunlight. The
swollen spot on his lip only makes him more handsome

in my eyes. "How did that poet you like so much—
Heine—put it? 'Think what world...'"

I take Father's hand and together, we recite the rest
of the poem: "Think what world is left you still, And
how lovely is that part."

Father is right. And though Heine lived long before
us, he knew it too. Even after all the senseless sorrow
and suffering, there is still world left. I know I will
never be able to forget all I saw and felt and lost in
Theresienstadt, but there is still world left.

It will be up to me to find the loveliness.

What World is Left was inspired by the experiences
of the author's mother, who was taken from Holland
to the concentration camp, Theresienstadt, where
this portrait was drawn by the Czech artist, Petr Kien.

Author's Note

A half-hour's drive north of Prague in the Czech Republic is an old, dreary-looking town called Terezin. It has a café on its main square and one small bed-and-breakfast.

But this place is haunted by ghosts. During the Second World War, when Germany occupied what was then Czechoslovakia, Terezin was known by its German name, Theresienstadt. Originally built as a garrison town in 1780 by Emperor Joseph II, and named for his mother, Empress Maria Theresa, it was used as a concentration camp during the Nazi regime. Many prominent Jewish European artists and musicians were among those imprisoned here.

Terezin was designed to house seven thousand soldiers. But during the Holocaust, the town had nearly ten times as many inhabitants. It is estimated that at its most crowded, there were four prisoners per square meter.

And yet, seen from a certain perspective, the prisoners who were sent here—mostly Jews, but also political prisoners—were the lucky ones. Though more than thirty thousand prisoners died in Theresienstadt, most of malnutrition and typhus, the camp was not a death camp like Sobibor or Auschwitz-Birkenau. There were no gas chambers.

In those bleak days, the trick was to find some way—any way—to remain in Terezin. This despite the watery broth prisoners lined up for at lunch and supper; the bedbugs and the lice; and the inhuman hours spent at tedious, often backbreaking, work. That was because Theresienstadt's inhabitants suspected—rightly—that to be sent on one of the frequent train transports east was worse.

Theresienstadt was also the scene of an elaborate hoax. In 1943, after the Danish Red Cross announced its plan to send a commission to visit the camp, the Nazi high command decided to gussy up the place. The work, known as the Embellishment, was carried out by prisoners, who built false storefronts, erected a monument and planted sapling poplars in the main square.

The Danish Red Cross commission was duped. As for the Nazis, they were so pleased with the success of their plan that, in 1944, they made a propaganda movie about the camp. Directed by Jewish German filmmaker Kurt Geron, the movie was called *The Fuhrer Gives a City to the Jews*. Its goal was to convince the world that Jews were prospering in the concentration camps.

My mother spent a little over two years in Theresienstadt. She, her two siblings and their parents survived thanks to my grandfather, Jo Spier, a Dutch artist who, among other tasks, made propaganda drawings for the Nazis. My mother was fourteen when she was sent to Theresienstadt; she was sixteen when the camp was liberated in 1945.

Until the winter of 2007, my mother never shared the story of her experience in Theresienstadt. But when the Conseil des Arts et Lettres du Quebec awarded me a grant to write a book based on my mother's wartime experience, my mother courageously agreed to revisit her past and share it with me—and by extension, you.

What World is Left is a work of fiction inspired by true events. Several of the scenes in this book are based on stories my mother told me. Others were inspired by an illustrated book my grandfather published in Dutch shortly before his death, entitled *Dat Alles Heeft Mijn Oog Gezien* [*All This My Eyes Have Seen*] (Elsevier, 1978).

I have made every effort to be historically accurate throughout *What World is Left*, but the central characters and their inner struggles are entirely imagined. For me, both as a reader and a writer, fiction is a way to help me make sense of the world and the people in it.

Montreal, March, 2008

Selected Bibliography

The Artists of Terezin. By Gerald Green. Hawthorne Books, 1969.

Ashes in the Wind: The Destruction of Dutch Jewry. By J. Presser. Trans. by Arnold Pomerans. Wayne State University Press, 1988.

Ghetto Theresienstadt. By Zdenek Lederer. Edward Goldston & Son Ltd., 1953.

I Never Saw Another Butterfly: Children's Drawings and Poems from Theresienstadt Concentration Camp 1942-1944. Edited by Hana Volavkova. Schocken Books, 1993.

In Memory's Kitchen: A Legacy From the Women of Terezin. Edited by Cara DeSilva. Trans. by Bianca Steiner Brown and David Stern. Jason Aronson, 1996.

Music in Terezin. By Joza Karas. Beaufort Books, 1985.

One Man's Valor: Leo Baeck and the Holocaust. By Anne E. Neimark. E.P. Dutton, 1986.

Seeing Through "Paradise": Artists and the Terezin Concentration Camp. Massachusetts College of Art, 1991.

The Terezin Diary of Gonda Redlich. Translated by Laurence Kutler. Edited by Saul S. Friedman. University of Kentucky Press, 1992.

Theresienstadt: Hitler's Gift to the Jews. Translated by Susan E. Cornyak-Spatz. Edited by Joel Shatzky. University of North Carolina Press, 1991.

University Over the Abyss: Lectures in Ghetto Theresienstadt 1942-1944. Verba Publishers, 2004.

Selected Websites

http://history1900s.about.com/library/holocaust/
aa012599g.htm (A virtual tour of modern-day Terezin.)

www.holocaust-trc.org

www.jewishvirtuallibrary.org/jsource/vjw/netherlands
(A virtual tour of Jewish history in the Netherlands.)

www.mhmc.ca (Montreal Holocaust Memorial Centre)

www.pamatnik-terezin.cz (The website for the Terezin
Memorial established in Terezin in 1947.)

www.ushmm.org (United States Holocaust Memorial
Museum)

In addition to writing novels for young adults, Monique Polak teaches English and Humanities at Marianopolis College in Montreal and is a frequent contributor to the Montreal *Gazette* and other Canwest publications across the country. Monique, who has a grown daughter, lives in Montreal with her husband. Visit her website at www.moniquepolak.com.